This is a work of fiction. Names, characters, places, and incidents either are the product of the author's imagination or are used fictitiously. Any resemblance to actual events, locales, organizations, or persons, living or dead, is entirely coincidental and beyond the intent of either the author or the publisher.

Masks Off!
TOP SHELF
An imprint of Torquere Press Publishers
PO Box 2545
Round Rock, TX 78680
Different Masks Copyright 2012 © by BA Tortuga, *Foxtrot* Copyright 2012 © by Missouri Dalton, *Believe Me, Beloved* Copyright 2012 © by Charlie Cochet, *As You Wish* Copyright 2012 © by Rob Rosen, *Alpha Prime* Copyright 2012 © by Katherine Halle, *What You Are* Copyright 2012 © by Elizabeth Brooks, *Annual Full Moon Werewolf Ball* Copyright 2012 © by Sean Michael.
Cover illustration by Alessia Brio
Published with permission
ISBN: 978-1-61040-352-8

www.torquerepress.com

Masks Off!

Masks Off!
edited by M. Rode

Torquere Press
Inc.
romance for the rest of us
www.torquerepress.com

Masks Off!

Table of Contents

Masks Off!

Foreword

There's something sexy about a masquerade, something hot in the mystery behind the mask, something intense in eyes shining through a disguise. We've taken all that and added an extra layer to the seductiveness of it—our heroes wear a facade beneath their mask—they're shifters.

This anthology offers you seven stories that explore what's beneath the masks that men wear, both figurative and literal. Humorous, hot, suspenseful, sexy, and yes, seductive: we hope you enjoy unveiling them all.

M. Rode

Masks Off!

Different Masks
by BA Tortuga

The air felt like he needed a machete to cut it. God, Lyons hated New Orleans in August. It sucked a man's soul right out of him.

Of course, he never went into the city unless he was on a retrieval, so maybe that was why he didn't like it. Most of the time it was depressing to track down a young loup-garou and haul them back to the pack. They always had such joy in testing their freedom and fought him so hard when the Alpha sent him to bring them home.

In this case, Lyons wasn't sad at all. He was fucking mad, and he was going to hunt Kipp's ass down and bring that fucker home.

Four months. Four months the little fuck had been gone. Just bugging out without a fucking goodbye or fuck you, or damn, that had been a wild night.

No, the man had just freaked out and left. Like they hadn't been best friends for damned near twenty years. Lyons growled, which made the street busker who'd been slipping up on him back off.

He caught a familiar scent, masked with grease and booze and... sugar?

He spun around, eyes moving over all the tables in Jackson Square—tarot readers and psychics and... There was an artist there at the corner, huge canvases of the full moon like a beacon.

Moving against the wind so it wouldn't carry his scent, Lyons moved around, trying to get a good look at the man, not the paintings.

Dressed in black with his hair slicked back and dyed dark, a sparkly glitter moon on one cheek, Lyon would never have recognized Kipp. The man was lean now, blue eyes sparkling in the streetlights.

He looked like he was incredibly happy.

It made Lyons want to kill him. Or at least beat him.

"Come and see la Luna, cheries. Come sample my wares."

The group of young ladies tittered and fluttered, Kipp's natural magic pouring out, drawing them in. That was cheating. Lyons was also pretty sure he didn't want anyone sampling Kipp's wares. In fact, those wares belonged to him, in his bed, sprawled out and begging, damn it.

His low growl wasn't loud enough for the human ear, but Kipp heard him. That pretty head snapped right up, those almost-gold eyes searching the square.

"I gotta go, y'all." The canvases were popped into a portfolio bag, then Kipp was running, moving toward the dark of the river.

That suited Lyons just fine. He did his best work in the dark, away from the lights and smells of human habitation. The river stank of pollution, but he could still follow Kipp's trail like it was a cartoon footprint.

Kipp wasn't stupid, though; the man zigzagged, then ducked into the French Market, moving fast.

Even if the market wasn't open, it was a fast corridor, and the food stalls were overwhelming. Lyons lost the trail for a second, stopping, trying to find that familiar scent.

He thought he'd lost it. He really did.

Then Kipp moved, the wind bringing Lyons that sugar/salt/male scent that screamed "mate" to him. He started moving again, glad he hadn't had to wolf out. People noticed way more these days.

Kipp was pushing it, sliding through the cemetery, the thugs looking for victims not even seeing him. Lyons put on speed, taking a chance and circling toward the west exit.

Kipp was barreling along the fence, looking for a place to go up and over. There wasn't much choice, though, not with the restoration they'd been doing. No, there was no way Kipp would avoid Lyons. No way at all.

Kipp slowed, rumbling softly, the sound worried, curious. Well, at least the man had no idea Lyons was the one after him. It wouldn't be curious if Kipp knew. It would be—should be—scared.

"What do you want?" The words were quiet, carried by Kipp's will.

He put on a little burst of speed, his hand closing on Kipp's arm. "I want you to come home, loup."

"Lyons?" Kipp stared at him, eyes huge. "The Alpha sent you?"

"Did you think he wouldn't? Sneakin' out like you did?"

Kipp's lips opened, then closed. "Just walk away. Please."

"No, loup. I ain't like you." He didn't want to just walk away, anyway. He wanted answers.

"No, you're not." Kipp's eyes moved over him, starving, desperate, so needy, and then the man shook his head, threw the bag of canvasses at him and leapt, scrambling over the fence.

By the time Lyons shouldered the bag and turned to follow, Kipp was gone.

***

Kipp hid in his rooms for three days before hunger drove him out.

Not physical hunger—although he needed a steak and something caffeinated—but psychic need. He fed on people's curiosity, their desire, anger. Even laughter. He wasn't in the pack where the energy floated everywhere, loose and free, so he had to feed here.

Lyons was out there, hunting him.

Kipp had no doubt that Girard had done it on purpose, sent his mate to fetch him home. The bastard had been furious to hear that he and Lyons were mated. Lyons was special, strong, and Girard fully intended Lyon to mate with someone—male or female—in the Alpha's line. Not one of the twitchy psys who lived on the fringe.

He'd left, knowing it was the only way to protect them both, protect his family, his mate. Himself.

He knew that Girard had sent Lyons to kill him because going back to the Pack meant death, and if Lyons killed him here instead...

Then the mate bond would be broken.

Too bad Kipp wasn't interested in dying.

He wasn't a danger to the pack. Why couldn't Lyons just go back and say the deed was done? Lyons was strong. He could forget in time, right?

Maybe Kipp should head west. Maybe up into the mountains. There were wolves there.

He was hiding today in tourist clothes, the temporary dye in his hair faded enough to look auburn now, the long tail of it tucked in the back of his shirt. Sunglasses and flip flops completed the masquerade, and he went to play.

Kipp sent a little prayer up to the lady moon that Lyons had given up, had moved on. Wandering down Royal from the Faubourg Marigny side toward the Quarter, he hummed a little, his body starting to feel alive again. Maybe he'd head toward Bourbon, get that steak.

It was blisteringly hot, baking his bones and making sweat pop up on his upper lip. That was a kind of food for his body in its own way. Made him feel alive.

He shopped, bumping elbows with tourists, humming under his breath.

Oh, masks. That mask shop was hardly ever open. He had to go in.

He slipped in, breathing in the scent of leather and paint. So yummy. The colors swirled together, all that glitter and plaster and paint like a drug. Mice and dogs, cats and moons, demons and dragons—the shapes fascinated him. The long noses on the plague doctor masks made his fingers itch to touch.

He reached out to stroke the tip of one of the masks, just the nose, when the shopkeeper tutted at him.

Damn it.

Kipp pulled back, stifling a sigh. He just needed the tiniest touch. All that energy the maskmaker poured into the piece would be his.

"How much is the mask? It's fascinating."

"Five hundred."

"Oh? Can I see it? Up close?"

"I'll get it down for you." The guy was giving him the stink eye, but that was okay. If he acted like a paying customer, the dude had to accommodate him.

The mask landed in his hand and the creative mojo hit him in a rush. Oh, better. "What's it made out of?"

"It's a traditional papier mache mold. The artist moved here from Venice. He apprenticed with the Boldrin brothers."

"Wow..." He handed it back, the look of respect on his face not faked in the least. "It's a beautiful piece."

He knew art. Hell, he'd lost a good thousand dollars

worth winging his portfolio at asshole's head in the cemetery.

"Thank you." The man's face softened into a smile for a moment. "You are truly an admirer."

"I am. One day, I'll have the cash for something this amazing."

"Well, come and see us when you do." The guy handed him a card. "Have you thought of apprenticing?"

"No. No, but... I work as an artist." It would be something new.

"I can tell about people. You should think about it."

"I will. Can I contact you for information?"

"Absolutely." The man came over and put a hand on his shoulder, a jolt of energy traveling all the way to Kipp's toes. Woo.

He had to close his eyes, the wolf wanting to see. "I'll be back, to talk to you."

"Good. Good. I'll look forward to it. I'm Philippe."

"Kipp." Philippe. He would remember.

Philippe smiled, a sharp, hungry expression, and turned away, letting Kipp slide out the shop door, his body buzzing with awareness.

Yum. God, he'd been so hungry without Lyons.

A hard body slammed into his, the speed shocking, leaving his body floating, his feet flying up into the air. He hit the wall of the alley next to the mask shop, brick crumbling around him a little.

"You let him touch you."

The world spun, Lyons' touch overloading him, Kipp's senses taking in the whole city for a heartbeat before focusing on his mate. "Let me go." He snapped at the air, letting his teeth show.

"No." Lyons' teeth closed on his throat, just like they had a right to.

Fuck.

Fuck.

His cock went hard so fast it hurt and he snarled, fingers tangling in Lyons' thick hair. He wasn't sure if he was pulling closer or away.

Lyons seemed far more certain, humping against him, thigh pushing between his to press against his crotch.

"Lyons. Fuck. We can't." Not here. Not like...

That knee nudged his balls and he convulsed, cried out, so close.

"We can. Come for me, pup, so I can take you to my room and fuck you so good."

"Lyons..." *Please. Please, mate.* His chin lifted, those teeth digging into his flesh again and he shot, his howl ringing out.

"Yes. Fuck, yes. Missed you." Lyons panted, head against his shoulder. "We need to move."

He nuzzled, filling his nose with that scent, the smell of home. "Lyons." He couldn't seem to say anything else.

"Oui, loup. Come on." Lyons took his hand in a firm grip, that hot, hot skin almost burning him.

He followed, his mind spinning, trying to find something not-Lyons to latch on to. There was nothing, not art or people or the oppressive heat, that could outshine Lyons in his consciousness.

Lyons dragged him into an alleyway and up a rickety set of stairs to one of those rent-by-the-week apartments for tourists. It was musty inside, making his nose twitch, but that was soon overpowered by the scent of Lyons' body, hot and male and perfect.

He reached for Lyons' shirt, nails digging in, tearing at it. Skin.

The broad, fuzzy chest was bare in moments, all that flesh there for him to love on.

He leaned in, caught Lyons' nipple in his teeth, tugging hard enough to feel. He wanted Lyons as crazy as he had been, wanted the man's hips to rock for him.

Lyons growled low, fingers in his hair, tugging the long braid from his shirt. His hair was dyed as dark as Lyons' now.

"I don't like it, loup. It's not right."

"I'm in hiding."

"You don't have to be." Lyons' hands slid up under his ass, lifting him, pulling him up.

Lyons had no idea. He'd explain. Later.

His legs wrapped around Lyons' waist, the solid strength like a column of heat. Lyons rubbed up on him, pushing him back against the wall. Those teeth latched onto his throat again, worrying the bruise there.

He was a mess, his pants wet, his throat throbbing, his disguise torn and mussed. Not that he gave a damn. When Lyons touched him, all he wanted was more.

His hair was pulled from the braid, the shorts torn from him and then his naked ass was rubbing against the painted wall.

Lyons held him up with one hand, skinning out of the tight jeans. That hard, hot cock pushed against him, right up under his balls.

"Mate..." He snapped at the air, the pressure like the best kind of tease.

"Want you, loup. Kipp. Mate." It was almost like Lyons was asking permission. Surely not.

"Yes." He needed. He could run, after. No one ever died from a good, hard fucking, right?

"Mine." Letting Kipp slide down, Lyons spun him around, pushing two wet fingers against his hole.

One hand was in the center of his back, holding him, helping him arch, offering his ass like a bitch in heat.

Lyons got him ready damned fast, fingers sliding inside him, opening him up. The burn made him snap, bite at the air, lightning sliding up his spine. His toes curled, his heels slamming against the floor to keep him upright.

"So tight. I swear, you're made for me, loup."

He knew it; that truth was burned in his soul. It'd damn near killed him to leave. He'd had his reasons, had known he could never do what the Alpha wanted.

Lyons' fingers pegged Kipp's gland, making him bark out his pleasure and surprise. Lyons' chuckle tickled his nape, his shoulders lifting with the sensation.

"Soon, hmm? Soon I'll fuck you until you scream for me."

"Need you, you bastard." More than his next breath.

"Thank the moon." The fingers inside him slid free, and Lyons moved up behind him, cock hard and hot and wet at the tip. He could feel it, pushing at his hole, demanding.

He bore back, refusing to let Lyons be in control of this, of everything. Damn it.

Lyons grunted, reaching down to grab Kipp's balls. "Mine, lover. All this is mine. You ever try to take it away again I'll--" Those teeth snagged the nape of his neck, worrying the skin there.

"Lyons!" The scar there burned, their bond flaring so brightly that the room darkened.

"Mmm." It was a growl, a sound of pure satisfaction. Lyons slid into him, filling him up, making him feel like he might burst with it.

The fingers around his sac were rough, the hand at his hip bruising as Lyons' teeth sank into his nape, holding him in place. That cock pushed inside him, then pulled out, making him feel almost raw.

His body jerked, his hole trying to keep Lyons in.

"Oh, fuck." Lyons started moving faster and faster. rocking against him, their skin slapping together.

Kipp bared his teeth, his claws on the wall as his mate took him. His head fell back a little, leaving the side of his neck open to those sharp teeth. Lyons took the opening, too, biting deep, shaking him and making it burn.

He barked out his need, his cock slapping his belly.

"That's it. Feels so good."

Good didn't begin to cover it. He slammed his hips back, taking Lyons to the root. Every movement made his cock swing, made his balls slide back and forth.

All he needed was a touch, one touch, but that son of a bitch wasn't giving it to him.

Lyons was like a machine, fucking him hard, sawing back and forth. Kipp needed more.

"Mate! Lyons! You bastard!" He tried to shift his weight, take them on one hand.

"No. You don't touch until I say."

Fucker. Beautiful, huge fucker.

Kipp swallowed down his whimper, tightening his ass, gripping that fat cock.

"Kipp." Finally. Finally Lyons reached down and grabbed his aching prick, stroking hard.

He went up on tiptoe, driving between fist and hips, snarling his pleasure. The whole world had gone black and white, his wolf right there at the edge of his consciousness.

Lyons snapped, vocalizing for him. Calling to him. His body tightened, his balls drawing up. All it took was Lyons' thumbnail dragging across his slit for him to lose it, seed spraying everywhere.

"Ugn." Lyons' hips snapped, pushing that sweet prick all the way in, and he felt it when Lyons let go. The man came for him like nothing going.

They stood together, panting, leaning against the wall.

Lyons licked the sweat from his neck. "My mate."

He groaned, deep in his chest, his world spinning, filled with Lyons.

Kipp knew he'd have to run again, have to get away.

Right now, though, he just wanted to feel Lyons' touch.

Just for a little while.

Lyons lay on top of Kipp, not letting the man so much as twitch without him knowing about it. He was supposed to take the man back to the pack, but he had a terrible urge to defy Girard and run, take Kipp far away.

Kipp was skinny and the hair was wrong, but the man's scent was right, and the way his pup slept like the dead was as familiar as breathing.

He grinned a little. He'd bet that Kipp hadn't been sleeping any more than he had since they'd been apart. Their mate bond was unusually strong, maybe because of Kipp's talents.

Kipp chirruped softly in his sleep, nuzzled his chest, words whispered without waking.

Stroking Kipp's hair, Lyons reached for the end of the braid, wanting to see it, even if wasn't the right color. It was supposed to be white-gold, but the black from three nights ago was red now. A few dozen washes and his pup would be right again.

That would be a fun job, honestly. Showering with his loup.

Kipp moaned, chin lifting to kiss him. "Lyons."

"Mmm. Bonjour, loup." Hello and good morning.

"Are you going to fuck me again before you kill me?"

The thought of killing Kipp made him want to snarl and bite, but not at Kipp. No. No matter what Girard said, he couldn't do that. "I'm not going to kill you, pup."

"Then what?" Kipp nuzzled his jaw. "I can't go back."

Lyons licked his lips, his cock rising. "Why not?"

"He'll kill me. That's why I left. You wouldn't think I'd just leave you behind, would you?"

"You just left. I didn't know."

Kipp leaned back, stared at him, eyes glowing. "I'm your mate. He told me you'd been promised to one of his kin. That if I didn't leave, he'd take me out."

Lyons' instinctive reaction was denial. Girard wouldn't do that to him. But he knew it had to be true. Kipp had never lied to him about pack rules.

"I'm not lying. If you came, killed me, you'd destroy the bond. I could lie and say I understand, but I don't."

He put his head down next to Kipp's, breathing in the scent of all that hair. "I never planned to kill you. I was going to take you home."

Girard was their Alpha. Theirs. Why would he have set them up?

"You'll have to go back without me."

"No." It came out without him even thinking about it. He couldn't go back without Kipp. It hurt, deep in his belly when they were separated.

Kipp groaned, nuzzled him. "You have to. I want you."

"Oh, loup, I want you, too. Not leaving without you." Of course, if what Kipp said was true, they couldn't just go home, either, could they?

"You're... how can you leave them? Girard wants you."

"I don't know why. He has plenty of support." It was just too weird.

"He wants you as part of his family. As his kin."

"I have a mate." That was all he needed to know right now.

He could smell how his words affected his pup, see those eyes flare. "Do you? Are you sure?"

"I am." He had no idea what that was going to mean for them, as he didn't think he could stay in the city and he was pretty sure they couldn't go back to the pack.

His pup said this was home, but... Kipp was too thin, needed to feed, to run. The pack was to the south; maybe they'd go north and east toward Texas. Find themselves a good territory.

Kipp leaned into him, nuzzled his jaw.

It was crazy, how fast he'd made his decision. "What do you need to be ready to go, babe? Girard will send someone else soon."

"What about your home? Your things? You're just walking away from them? From the Pack?"

"If Girard intends to break our mate bond I don't have a choice. I'm not losing you."

Kipp looked at him, utterly stunned. He couldn't decide if it was adorable or infuriating that Kipp honestly believed that he would follow orders and not his mate bond. Lyons hated to think he'd been that much of an ass over the years. Then again, maybe he hadn't been the one to make Kipp think that way.

"What all do you need, loup? We have to get moving."

"I have supplies, things, not much. Just a room." Kipp shrugged. "It's hard, in a city."

"I know." He hated it. His neck felt like rock, his belly queasy. "Well, we'll gather up your things, and I have your art."

"Good. It's worth a little money. Enough."

"It's yours." He'd never really understood Kipp's thing, his psychic gift and art and all, but it was part of Kipp, and that was enough for Lyons. He smacked Kipp's hip lightly. "Up. We'll move on and have each other again once we've cleaned up our trail."

It was tough to do, because he wanted Kipp like he wanted his next breath.

"That long?" Kipp kissed him, long and slow, tongue fucking his lips, his mate gone all sex-kitten.

Oh, fuck. How could he resist that? He pressed Kipp

back, taking the kiss to a whole new level.

Those hands were all over him, tugging him closer, dragging him in against that lean, hard body. Somebody must like the idea of them going away together, just the two of them. Lyons had to admit he liked it when Kipp took off like a bottle rocket.

Kipp wrapped around him, moaned deep, teeth leaving little bites all over his shoulders, his chest. He moaned, rolling up so he could press them together all the way, from lips to hips. He needed everything.

"Need you. Need to feel." Desperate man. Hungry pup.

"I know. I know, loup." Lyons was just as needy. Damn Girard for his fucking plans, anyway.

Kipp's cock left burning wet kisses on his skin, fingers digging in hard enough to bruise. His pup had never been so forceful. It felt amazing.

He rolled Kipp beneath him, growling, his teeth at the long throat.

"Mate." Kipp yelped, body arching impossibly. His. His.

"Yes." He pushed between Kipp's legs once more, his cock hard, almost too sensitive, his balls drawing up.

Kipp thrust up restlessly, cock slipping against his belly, their hips slapping together.

Gritting his teeth, he pulled back enough to set his cock at the tight hole, the head sliding right into Kipp's body. Kipp never even slowed, that tight body slammed down, took him in to the fucking root, and he couldn't fight his howl.

He threw his head back, his growls ringing out as he slammed home, his body bucking. "Kipp."

The bed frame screamed, but Kipp didn't back off, just took him harder. They moved together, rocking, grunting, rutting. Sweat dripped off his body, and his skin felt too tight.

"Yours. Yours." Kipp's claws raked down his chest, marking him.

"Mine, loup. Always mine."

"Always." The word was almost a sob.

"Yes." He gritted his teeth, sawing back and forth.

Kipp's eyes went wide, the wolf there suddenly, sharp and perfect, reflected in pure gold.

Lyons growled, his body going wild, his orgasm raw and harsh and perfect. He came inside Kipp's body so hard the world dissolved into white noise.

His pup was panting in his arms when the room coalesced, spunk drying between them. Lyons took a hard kiss, mashing their lips against their teeth. It seemed important to imprint on his mate right now, right at this moment.

Kipp moaned for him, holding on tight, eyes squeezed shut.

"Shh. I got you, loup. I got you."

"Yeah." Kipp licked his jaw, loving him. "Love, huh?"

"Oh, yeah. Love you, pup. Never doubt it." He'd just given up his pack for Kipp without really even a whimper.

"Not once. I swear." Kipp's hands stroked his spine, petting him, easing him down.

They needed to move on. They really did. So why was it he only wanted to take another nap?

Kipp rumbled softly, humming for him, and he melted. His mate. That was all he needed.

The rest of them could just fuck off.

Kipp threw everything he could in a bag, cussing himself the entire fucking time.

Asshole Pack.

Asshole Girard.

Asshole him.

Lyons was willing to leave it all, give up everything the man had—home, family, status, security—and for what?

Him?

He had been a shit choice before this. Now he wasn't anybody.

And he was supposed to just let Lyons become an outcast? Shit. He didn't think so.

Right?

"You can't do that to him, Kipp. You can't. He's got a home. People that will make it better. You can't fuck anything else up." He figured if he said it all the way to Texas it would work.

He'd left a note in that rickety room that he knew would be his last memory of his mate. It was simple. It just said, "You can go home now."

"This fucking sucks hairy monkey mole balls." He dragged his fingers through his hair, the mass wild and tangled, the scent of Lyons on him.

"You think? I think that may be too small, loup."

He dropped his bag. "Lyons? You are *supposed* to be asleep!" He'd magicked the man, for fuck's sake.

"Mmm. Imagine that. My mate is psychic, did you know?" Lyons was smiling. That was always dangerous.

Kipp stamped one foot on the ground. "You have to... I can't do this with you looking at me! It's not natural, to be good! Twice in a row! I..." He pursed his lips. "Turn around."

"Nope." Lyons advanced, the grin widening. "I'm gonna help you pack, pup."

"You have to stay over there."

Lyons. Lyons. Lyons. The man's energy poured over him like a levee breaking.

"No, I don't. You're not leaving without me." Lyons touched him, and it was like a live wire hit his arm.

He barked, his tail wanting to wag, his eyes crossing. No fair. Lyons wasn't psychic or anything, but he was Kipp's mate, after all. Therefore, he was impossible to resist.

And it was Lyons, his solid, sure Lyons. "I didn't want you to lose everything, love."

Lyons snorted. "Oh, now, loup-garou. You know me. I don't take long to adjust." Lyons reeled him in for a kiss. "I just want to get a head start on Girard's next henchman. Texas sounds good."

"I like Texas. They have barbecue." He rubbed their cheeks together, groaning. "Anywhere is good."

He'd used up all the good in him, in walking out the door and leaving Lyons sleeping. All of it.

"Then let's finish packing you. I brought your art." Lyons kissed him again, then popped his butt.

"No swacking." He nipped the air, almost playfully.

"No mind-whammy, then."

"Mind-whammy? Me?" He didn't whammy anyone.

Usually.

Unless he needed to.

"None." Lyons moved around, gathering up his things, not having to ask which were important.

He helped, grabbing his pillow, Gram's photo album. They were really doing this.

"We are, loup. You and me." Lyons slung a bag over one shoulder. "Ready?"

"You know I am." Lyons knew him, bond deep.

"Well, come on, then." They headed out into the street, and he realized he didn't know if Lyons had come in a vehicle or if he'd come on foot.

"Will he chase us?" His fingers touched the small of Lyons' back.

Lyons' mouth pressed into a flat line. "He'll send someone. I'll deal with it."

"I... You could go back. No one would know." He wasn't going to offer again. He would bite Lyons if his mate agreed. It just seemed like the right thing to do.

"Where are you taking him, Lyons? Are you bringing him home?" Girard stood in front of them by an alley, flanked by two others.

"He is." Kipp lifted his chin. "He found me." *Don't be scared. Don't be scared.* He wasn't sure if he was talking to himself or Lyons.

Lyons threw him a look that could only be called incredulous. "No, Girard. I'm not bringing him back. You want him dead."

Girard shrugged. "We have plans for you, friend. A better pairing."

Kipp refused to wince.

Lyons growled, the sound low, menacing. "This is my mate."

"That can be rectified."

Kipp snarled softly, bared his teeth. "Fuck you."

"I don't think you understand." Girard's eyes flashed gold, the Alpha right there, and Kipp's body wanted to step back. He didn't. "You're my pack."

"You sent me away. You separated a bonded pair. You don't deserve to be an Alpha." Kipp knew his ass was toast.

Lyons touched Kipp's shoulder, and he could feel his mate's pride as Lyons spoke. "You lied to me, G."

"You have better things in your future than a crazy asshole from the fringes."

"I'm not an asshole."

"Kipp is my mate, and I don't want anything else." Lyons stepped in front of him now.

"You don't get a choice, Lyons. This is my pack."

"Are we really going to have a pissing contest here on the street?" Kipp was fairly sure that was a shitty idea.

"You want me to piss up in your rented room?" Girard bared his teeth. The two with him shifted from foot to foot.

"No. I want you to go home and be happy and let us go to Texas, but you're an ass and you're not going to let this be that easy." Kipp knew he had diarrhea of the mouth, but he couldn't stop.

Lyons snorted, the sound amused as hell. "You gonna take me down, Brandon? What about you, Tru?"

Tru looked away, but it was Brandon whose eyes rolled. "Girard, let them go, man. Lyons don't want to come home."

"I need him."

Lyons grinned at Brandon, which made Kipp wonder if there was something there he didn't know about. He'd really never known Lyons' friends. "Let Brandon marry your sister, man."

Girard growled as Brandon chuffed softly. "I brought your stuff, buddy. A guy needs his stereo and shit."

"Thanks." Lyons nodded, then glared at Girard. "You don't need me, man. You need to get with the times, though, or you'll lose more than me and Kipp." Look at his Lyons, being all evolved.

Kipp nodded. Let them go. Really. They were harmless.

Girard growled, but it was Tru who touched the Alpha's arm. "They don't want to come home, G. Let them go. There's not enough of us to risk."

Dude. That worked.

There was something about Tru's touch that made Girard relax, and when Tru finally met Kipp's eyes, there was complete understanding there. Oh. Oh, he'd never known Tru was like him.

"You ever expose us, you're dead," Girard finally growled. "Give him his shit, Brandon."

Brandon nodded, the relief clear on the man's face,

and a set of keys were tossed over. "You're parked off Decatur."

Lyons reached out to shake hands with Brandon, then Tru. He held a hand out to Girard, as well. "Thanks."

"You're making a mistake. You could have everything."

Kipp had taken all he could. "He has me. That's all he needs. You go make babies or something!"

Lyons soft laughter tickled his shoulder. "You tell them, loup."

He thought he had. God, the big alpha males were so confusing sometimes.

Girard didn't make nice. He just turned on his heel and left, and Kipp had to admit, the air whooshed out of his lungs with relief.

He looked at Lyons, just a little freaked. "So, that went well."

Lyons blinked at him, then laughed, the sound a little rusty but good, like old water pipes. "Yeah. I'd say it went as well as we could expect."

"It'll be good now?" He wanted to go, to drive, maybe have a hamburger.

"It will, at least for right now." Lyons pulled him into the shadows next to the door to kiss him hard. "Looks like Tru was on your side."

"Looks like. Don't tell on him." They weren't welcome, witchy wolves. Everyone had their own masks to wear.

"Oh, loup, I wouldn't say a word. Let's go, hmm? My truck will be where Brandon said."

It still amazed Kipp that Lyons would leave the pack for him, just like that.

The fingers at the small of his back moved, made his eyes cross. "Yes, loup. Just like that."

Kipp panted. "Stop reading my mind. That's my job."

Lyons laughed, the sound becoming easier, smoother every time it happened. "Nope. Your job now is to keep me busy. You have to make up for the whole pack."

"I can do that. I'm made to do that."

After all, he could always tempt Lyons to sleep.

Masks Off!

Foxtrot
By Missouri Dalton

Cacophonous music beat counterpoint to the throbbing of my head. I pressed the sweating glass of scotch on the rocks against my forehead and sighed. Coming here had been a terrible idea from the start. The hard plastic edge of my mask dug into my forehead. I could see a foggy reflection of myself in the mirror over the bar.

The mask covered from my eyebrows down, over my thin, pointed nose and across sharp cheeks to sweep down to my acute jaw line leaving a rounded opening where my mouth was free. Amber eyes—fox eyes—stared out of the steel-toned mask. The chick at the shop where I'd bought said it was a reproduction of some Carnivale mask from Venice. I just thought it was cool—and had the benefit of covering nearly my whole face. My hair stuck up all over my head normally, ginger spikes that made me look like a damn porcupine. I'd slicked it down tonight in an attempt to look more put together.

I'd even worn something outside of my usual job attire, jeans and a blazer, and opted for a white linen suit. Very old South meets Jersey mafia. I stood out like a fucking apple in a bowl of oranges. But I was unrecognizable, and that was what mattered.

Joker, the bartender, a monstrously huge fellow with

dreadlocks and the sort of face only a mother could love, leaned over the bar and stared at me. "You look like hell, Fawkes."

"Fuck you." I downed my scotch; the cold of the ice made my teeth ache. "Why am I here?"

"You agreed to come." Joker was the only person in the club *not* wearing a mask. It was Hide's annual Halloween Masquerade. I wasn't personally into the leather scene, but Joker had asked me to come, so I came. I owed him a few favors.

"I did. When's my next set?" I was entertainment for the crowd. I'd run one set earlier in the evening already. My saxophone case was on the counter next to me. I ran a hand over the leather, trying to find comfort in the familiar. I hadn't been avoiding the club just because I wasn't into the scene; I'd been avoiding it because *he* was here. All the time. So immersed in this world he'd had no time for mine.

Ending things over the phone hadn't been the grown up thing to do, but I hadn't wanted to meet him in person. My desire to tear his throat out was too high after he cheated on me. I'd been around too long to waste time on cheating bastards.

To be fair, it wasn't all his fault that things between us hadn't worked out. I was to blame for some of it. He wasn't prepared to follow me down the fox-hole into my fucked up world. He wasn't ready to see the world that lies right next to his.

I could sense them, the predators that were more than human, roving through the club. Vampires that took the very scent of the air away with them, *versi* with the scent of forest and blood clinging to them, elfkin like Joker that smelled of magic and rainwater, and the odd adept— human but stinking of power.

Joker knew what I was, protected my secret from

the others. I wasn't the last of my kind, but it had been decades since I had met another of us—and there were too many who would kill first and ask questions later. No one trusted vulpes.

"Remy."

"Huh?"

"I said ten-thirty," Joker replied. "You were spaced."

"Sorry." I moaned and restrained myself from running my hands through my hair. "I'm so out of it, Jo."

"No problem. Masks off at midnight. You'll want to wrap before that."

I nodded. The mask kept me from being recognized. I didn't want him to know I was here. Or any other former flames, for that matter. Hide's Masquerade drew lots of folks from the supernatural set, and I'd dated a few of them over the years. None of those relationships had gone very well, either. Masks off at midnight was a tradition. The normals had about an hour after that to get the hell out of Dodge before things got wild.

"Can I have another?" I waved my glass at him. "I have a headache."

"Fine. Last one."

"Okay." I watched him pour and tried to concentrate on the sound of the clear gold liquid splashing down around the half-melted ice cubes. It was hard to be in a loud room like this. My ears were too sharp. The music was the only thing anchoring me. Music always anchored me. It's something vulpes are good at besides lying and stealing.

Joker left me with my drink to help a struggling bartender. I wrapped my hand around the glass and tapped a counter beat against the surface with my nails. I had ten minutes before I needed to set up. Turning away from the bar, I took a look out over the crowd. Writhing bodies danced to the quick tempo of drums and electric guitar. The latest band of the evening was up on stage already. I wasn't a fan of the beat, but the boy they had on lead guitar wasn't bad, neither was the lead singer. It was a Goth sort of band, a little bit punk. The logo on the drum read *Sweet Malady*. They would be an interesting act to follow.

To be honest, when Joker had asked me to play here, I was surprised. I was a jazz man these days. This was *not* a jazz sort of club. I'd give it a go, though. Put a little heart into it.

I finished my drink and started to get down off the bar stool when a smell struck me like a freight train. It cut through the scents of sweat and blood and bodily fluids. I looked to Joker. He'd noticed it as well.

It was a versi. A wild one. The kind that killed people for sport judging by the sort of acrid, rotting odor attached to his personal musk.

I headed for the stage and struck up an innocent conversation with the sound manager until I could set up. I could still smell him, definitely a him, but he wasn't getting any closer. After agreeing on the mike placement with the sound manager, I set my case down and assembled the saxophone, sliding the bracing strap over my neck and snapping the instrument into place.

I sighed, staring at my shoes. They were white, too, like my suit. The lighting manager had already changed the lighting. I got a simple spot light, none of those weird strobes that made my brain twitch.

If I didn't owe Joker, I would be out of here. I had no desire to run into a wild versi.

Putting it out of my mind, I headed on stage after a quick introduction from the previous act's lead singer. While I played my set it was easy to get lost in the music. I could block everything else out. As I played, the tone of the club changed.

That's what happened when vulpes played music. Our emotions transferred out into the melody. The more heart I put into the music, the more effect I would have on the crowd. I chose not to do that, however. I didn't want to show my hand, as it were.

It was about eleven fifteen when I wrapped up. Half an hour wasn't a long set, but there was another band on after me for the midnight unmasking. I got my things together and made my way back to bar to let Joker know I was lighting out of here.

"Nice playing," someone remarked. I turned to get a look at the speaker. He was wearing a harlequin mask with black and red diamonds and gold detailing. It looked expensive. Pitch black curls brushed the top of the mask and stuck out all over his head. He was taller than me, but practically every fucking guy I met was taller than me. At five foot four, I was short. I knew I was short. I also knew that every man I dated over the years looked like he was robbing the cradle.

Most vulpes were short. I'd never met one taller than five foot nine, and he'd been the tallest I'd ever seen. My mother had been around five three, and of the kits she had birthed, I was the tallest and the only one still alive. I'd had a brother and two sisters; they'd been killed when we were just starting to tumble out of the burrow. I still had nightmares about that day. What those fucking *versi* thought a bunch of kits could do I don't know, but I'd avoided them like the plague ever since—except for one time a couple years ago with a rather attractive specimen. I'd been incredibly drunk.

And this well-dressed fellow in the expensive mask smelled all over of wolf. The hair on my arms rose a bit, and I had to clamp down to prevent a little croak from escaping my lips. I recognized the scent, the shape of his hands. Those lips.

"It's Remy, right? I'd recognize that figure anywhere."

Okay, so perhaps the mask wasn't enough to completely mask my identity. I had to start considering relocating. I mean really, clearly I was way too used to Chicago. And Chicago was way too used to me, for that matter.

"Jonathon," I replied. "It's been ages." I tried to put on a cheerful air, but was not entirely successful.

He smiled, his dark eyes glinting behind the mask. "I was hoping I would run into a familiar face here. Most of these fellows are a bit too earnest for my taste."

"I have to agree. This isn't my scene." I set my instrument case down. "So why are you here?"

"I was in town chasing a warg and decided to socialize with the local pack. They recommended this party as a way to let off steam."

Warg. That's what I'd smelled earlier on, but I didn't smell it now. I guess Jonathon got his beastie.

"Wait until midnight, things will get wild then," I said.

"Oh really?" He moved closer and leaned over me. "And what if I want things to get wild sooner?"

I may have just broken up with Bjorn, literally having called him with the news this morning, but I recovered quickly from things like that. You learned to roll with the punches after your eighth decade or so. So Jonathon's less than subtle invitation was more than welcome.

Even if he was a damn versi.

"I hear there are all sorts of rooms tucked away downstairs." He leaned in closer, touching my mask. "Hidden places." His voice took on a distinctly husky tone that set goose bumps to rise across my skin.

The only problem with saying yes to Jonathon was his expectation of how I would behave. It had been at least fifteen years since we'd been together. Fifteen years ago I'd been a different person. More adventurous in my sex life for certain. Jonathon and I had even gone hunting together. He was a rare sort of versi; he'd never cared what I was.

But that hadn't turned into a long term relationship. I had no problem fooling around with him now, though.

"Sure, let's go exploring," I smiled. "I'm in the mood for hidden places. Let me put my saxophone behind the bar, and we'll go."

"Sure thing, sweetheart." He leaned down and gave me a quick kiss. The buzzing sensation left on my lips in the aftermath was pleasant and sent warm little waves radiating from my lips and my heart beating faster.

I hurried back to the bar, motioning to Joker before setting the case down on the counter. "Watch this for me, won't you?"

He nodded, and I headed back to Jonathon. "Lead on."

Jonathon smiled and put an arm around my shoulders. "Just like old times."

Yeah, old times. I could drown myself in Jonathon and forget all about Bjorn. That would be for the best. Jonathon wasn't entirely certain which way we were going, but it didn't entirely matter, because I did. Joker and I going back as far as we did, I'd been to Hide and had ample time to explore during non-business hours. He usually let me hide out in the twisty sub-basement whenever someone was after me. A more recent incident involving me pissing off a troll had led to this favor actually.

We headed down into the dungeon-like sub-basement to find an empty room. There was a lot going on down here. Men and men, women and men, women and—whatever the hell that thing was, intertwined in a dance of lust and self-esteem issues with the addition of whips and collars.

Props. I'd never found any of those things necessary

to show someone how I felt. I suppose there were those who found it necessary. I understood. They were hoping that it would let them strip away the mask they wore, or put one on. It gave them a way to be honest in a way they couldn't be otherwise.

I needed none of that to strip away my mask. I could shed this skin for another in the space of a heartbeat—I could be something new and powerful. I needed no props. Bjorn had. He couldn't understand my dislike of it, either. When I tried to explain I was part wild animal and no matter how domesticated I might have become I couldn't stand to be restrained, it fell on deaf ears.

So I changed for him. I showed him what I was, and he-- he cheated on me with that. *That.* Just thinking about it pissed me off. I located an empty room with haste, pulling Jonathon inside.

He growled in encouragement, pulling the door closed behind us and slipping out of his jacket. "I'm so glad I ran into you, Remy. I forgot how much I missed a little fox now and then."

"I'm glad you ran into me, too." I pulled my mask off; the skin on my face welcomed the air. The small room we had found occupancy in was equipped with a low mattress strewn with pillows and decorated in a sort of harem style.

I found myself on the mattress pretty damn fast. That was one problem with being slight. In spite of being stronger and faster than my size might otherwise indicate, I couldn't compete with the strength of a versi twice my size.

I shed my jacket and tie and was tangled up in his arms before I could catch my breath. I had missed *this.* Being caught up in the arms of someone who truly understood what I was, what I could take. His hands were big and calloused. His lips still remembered the little spot behind my ear that drove me crazy.

I still remembered things about him, too.

I was enraptured when the door to our little room banged open. I heard Jonathon say something and pulled myself out of my daze to see what was going on. A tall, slender shouldered man stood framed in the doorway, one hand flung out to hold the door open and the other clutching the frame. He wasn't wearing a mask.

His vibrant red hair was sleek, his gray suit tailored to fit, and his tie the same green as his eyes. There were freckles on his crooked nose. A small scar tugged at the corner of his lips—it hadn't been there the last time I'd seen him.

Ian. He and I had a thing once, years ago, but seeing him still made my heart beat faster.

"What the hell are you doing?" I demanded, pulling myself free of a pillow and Jonathon's left leg. I pulled my shirt closed and tried not to blush like a virgin caught by his parents.

"I'm afraid I need to borrow you, Remy."

"Uh--"

Jonathon got to his feet and faced off with Ian, who was shorter than him. The slender redhead had a few tricks up his sleeve Jonathon couldn't know about, but I couldn't think of a way to warn him off.

"Look, I don't care who you are, get the fuck out of here," Jonathon snarled.

Ian took one look at the versi and punched him square in the jaw. Jonathon went down, and Ian calmly stepped over him and looked assessingly at me. I waited for Jonathon to get back up, but he didn't.

"Jonathon? Are you okay?"

"He'll be fine," Ian reassured. The man stooped over and picked me up, slinging me over his shoulder like a sack of flour.

I did not take it kindly. "Put me down!" I kicked and thrashed and was tempted to go for his throat.

He clamped one arm down on my legs. Stronger than normal, I was. Stronger than him? Not so much. I had to stop dating men so much bigger than me. Clearly there was some deep-seated psychological problem I was suffering from to cause this preference, but it ended now, damn it. Ian quickly carried me down the hall and upstairs to the main room. I don't know what he thought he was doing, and I was having little success with non-lethal extraction.

When we got to the bar, he set me down on a stool and gestured to Joker, who brought over a pair of drinks. Ian smiled and took them, handing one to me.

"So, how is my little fox?"

"What the hell, Ian? I was *busy*." And we hadn't dated in twenty years, what was he thinking?

"Sorry about that, kid, but I need a favor. Actually, Cormac needs a favor."

Fuck me. Cormac? King of the elves and pain in everyone's ass. "Why?" I'll admit it, I whined.

"Tonight is also the night of *his* annual masquerade, as you well know." He took a sip of the strangely red colored drink in his hand. Mine was scotch. I had no idea what was in his. I wasn't sure I wanted to know.

"Yes, I know." I drank. I had a feeling I'd want to be drunk for this.

"His midnight entertainment cancelled, and I thought of you. Cormac is so fond of jazz music, and you are the best," he flattered. "I'm certain he would be *very* grateful."

I was certain that if I said no I would end up dead somewhere. "Fine. I'll get my sax and we'll go." I gulped down the rest of my drink. "But you owe me, *big*."

"Of course." He smiled. It wasn't much of a smile. Ian didn't really do real smiles. I couldn't really blame him. Cormac had Ian tied tightly around his finger, a cautionary tale for anyone who did business with the elf king, and Ian had lost a lot of loved ones because of it.

I wondered what it was like for a human being to live as long as Ian had, watching everyone he loved die one after the other. It was the reason we hadn't really worked out; he had never gotten over his first love. It had been more than fifty years since Billy died, but the years didn't matter much to Ian.

I grabbed my saxophone, and we headed out of the bar to Ian's waiting car. The black limo had a driver in the front seat. Ian got into the back with me, placing a comforting hand on my shoulder. There were three white boxes on the seat across from us.

"Cormac sent things for you to wear," Ian gestured to the first two boxes. "And a mask."

I opened the smaller box first and sighed. "Seriously?" The mask was a fox. Well made of molded leather and hand painted with gilt detailing.

"You know how he is."

"Yeah, yeah." I grabbed the other box. A ginger-toned tweed suit. I sighed and started stripping off the rest of my clothes. I had no qualms about changing in front of Ian.

"New scars," he remarked when I took my shirt off.

I looked down at my torso. I'd had a few scraps since I'd seen him last. "You know me, always making new friends." I'd always had scars. There were three thin marks that ran from my cheek down my jaw and stopped halfway down my neck. Claw marks. My brother had done it in his death throes. I touched them reflexively, and Ian caught my hand.

"I'm sorry," he said.

"Not your fault." I wanted to pull my hand away, but didn't. I'd loved Ian. I think part of me still did. But how could I compete with Billy?

He pulled my hand toward him, turning it to kiss my palm. My heart beat sped up. I tried to calm down, tried to let the hum of the engine and the sounds of the city passing by us meld into music, but it wasn't working.

"The driver can't hear us," he whispered. "I have to confess, seeing you with that werewolf made me a little jealous. I thought you were with some big Scandinavian." His soft, Dublin drawl reminded me of cello music. A soft baritone smoother than fifteen-year-old scotch.

"He cheated on me—with a vampire," I replied. "Dumped his ass."

"Oh, my poor fox." He kissed my wrist. Butterflies took flight in my stomach. Ian had that effect on me. He smelled like sunshine and green growing things. "All alone in the city." He tugged me close to him and kissed me full on the lips.

I wanted to melt right there. "Ian..." I tried to remember that this was a bad idea. We'd both regret it later. I couldn't replace Billy, and he couldn't replace the family I'd lost.

"Shh. It doesn't matter tonight." He kissed me again. "Have you ever had sex in a limo?"

I grinned. "No."

"Well then, here's your chance." His hands went for my belt, and I kicked off my shoes. I had a sudden irrational hatred for pants. They took too long to get off of me. Ian seemed to know I wasn't in the mood for slow and romantic. The heat in me set the smell of wild off of my skin. I couldn't help it. Ian took that as his cue.

This was wild. Teeth and taste of blood. I dug my nails into his back and nipped at his neck and chest. Our breath clouded the windows, and sweat made the leather beneath us slick. I sweat easily. Ian came, and I followed soon after with a wild bark that wasn't anywhere near human.

I panted and gave into my desire to lick his face to taste the sweat there. He tasted like me. I nuzzled my head against his chin and made a contented huff.

"The party," he whispered. "We have to get dressed."

I realized then that the limo was no longer moving. "Fuck."

"There are towels," he said. "Don't worry."

While Ian fiddled with something on the other side of the limo, I pulled myself into a sitting position and stretched. I'd needed that. If I'd been a cat, I would have been purring.

Towels were forthcoming, and we cleaned up before I got dressed. The suit fit like a glove, no surprise there, it was clearly fairy make. Tiny fucking stitches. There were leaping foxes embroidered around the cuff and collars of the cream colored silk shirt.

"Please tell me I get to keep the clothes." I luxuriated in the silk with a grin. You didn't get fairy made clothes very often these days.

"Part of the package," Ian confirmed. "He's also agreed to a boon."

I paused in my admiration of the clothes and raised my eyebrows. "Seriously?"

Ian nodded.

That was... That was a big deal. Cormac granted a boon perhaps once a year. He must be desperate for entertainment. "Who did he have originally for this soirée?"

"Niada."

I found myself surprised again. "The siren? Why couldn't she make it?"

"Apparently she lost her voice and is having some trouble finding it. Something about a wizard and a seashell—I wasn't really listening." He pulled a pack of cigarettes from his pocket. "Do you mind?"

"Go ahead." I got the pants and suit jacket on before grabbing the amber silk tie patterned with more foxes. There was a pocket square and a pair of brown leather shoes.

Ian finished half his cigarette in the time it took me to get finished dressing. There was still a box left unopened.

"What's that?" I asked.

"My mask," he replied, putting the cigarette out in a small ashtray built into the wall of the limo. He leaned over to pick up the box. "Cormac picked it out." He opened the box to let me look. It was a Comedy mask. "He says it's the only way he can get me to smile."

"He is an ass."

"You would be right." He sighed. "Come on then, he's surely expecting us." He checked the time. "It's already ten to midnight." He tied my mask for me, and I returned the favor before we headed inside the Hilton, residence of the elf king. People tended to be surprised when they found out he lived in a hotel. They ought to see his place in Faerie, that place looked straight out of a little girl's fantasy. I'd seen it once when I first swore fealty to the elf king.

I had sort of hoped that would be the last time I ever saw him.

The elves guarding Cormac's door didn't so much as give us a second glance, but then, I was with Ian, and Cormac trusted Ian more than he trusted himself. The dimensions of the room I entered off the hallway were in no way in keeping with the reality of the hotel. I could feel the edges of Fairie. The holiday was making it easier for this sort of merging to occur. Cormac had pulled the ballroom of his palace into the hotel. The huge room had no ceiling, opening up on a starry sky with constellations unknown to man.

The gilded walls were lit with will-o-wisps in orange

and gold; huge pumpkins carved with scenes from fairy stories were placed all around the room. Pixies flittered about the air and everywhere I looked were fey creatures of every description.

I was the only vulpe in the room. I clutched my saxophone tight and tried to remember that Cormac didn't murder people in public.

Cormac himself appeared out of the crowd, flashy in a gold suit. He had a very delicate, practically lacy, gold mask on that didn't hide his identity in the slightest. The crown of his office, a gold wire creation studded with fairy lights and diamonds, winked and sparkled. He was the most striking thing in the room, and he knew it.

"Remy," he greeted. "So happy you could make it!"

I bowed deeply. "Your majesty."

"I have a place arranged for you. I'm sure Ian has told you I adore jazz."

"Yes, your majesty."

"We'll have masks off at one. Be sure to play something cheery."

"Yes, your majesty."

"All right then, Ian, be a dear and show Remy his place. I have so many guests to attend to."

Ian nodded and watched the king leave before rolling his eyes, the only feature of his I could see for the mask. "He's in fine form tonight. Cheerful even. Walk lightly."

"Will do." I followed him through the crowd of dancing fey to a small stage set up in the far corner of the ballroom. There wasn't any microphone, but I had no concern about being heard. I set up quickly and was forced to push the mask up onto the top of my head in order to play. Cormac clearly hadn't thought that through entirely.

I started with slow jazz to set the tone of the room before moving to some of the swing numbers from the twenties and thirties. Midnight came and went, and when the time for unmasking rolled around I picked up the tempo as requested. It was always best to oblige Cormac.

The night wore on and ethereal bonfires began to appear around the floor. Per tradition, Cormac took the arm of his queen, an elf woman whose name I had never learned, and leapt over the fire with her. Other couples were quick to follow suit and before long the fey creatures were slipping out of the ballroom and into the night.

Masks littered the glittering marble floor of the empty ballroom. I had stayed out of the pairing. It was a fertility tradition, and I wasn't exactly contributing to the gene pool. I took a deep breath and tracked down water at a long table of refreshments now abandoned.

I helped myself to some food and took a seat on the floor after clearing away some masks.

"Well, that was practically tame for Samhain," Ian said, pulling on a cigarette.

"You not up for a roll in the dirt?" I raised my eyebrows. "I thought Cormac would have insisted."

"He knows better." Ian sat down next to me. "I've already got a family to look after. My granddaughter is in rehab."

"Rose, right? She would be...eighteen now. Right?"

He nodded. "They grow up so fast. Just yesterday I feel like she was a toddler. Now she's a beautiful young woman plagued by visions with a heroin addiction."

"Jesus."

He punched me on the shoulder. "Don't say the Lord's name in vain."

I snorted. "You never change, do you? We make quite a pair. You're morbidly unhappy, and I'm a pariah stuck dating the bottom of the barrel because one fucking vulpe decided to lure off a bunch of kids and eat them." Fucking Pied Piper.

"You want a hug?"

"Yeah." I scooted close to him and leaned against him. He wrapped an arm around me. "This is sort of pathetic, isn't it?"

"Oh, I don't know, it could be worse."

"Oh?"

"I could be sitting here with Cormac instead of an adorable fox." He kissed my cheek. "You said you loved me once, before we called it quits."

"I did."

"Maybe I can't replace Billy—but maybe—maybe it's time I moved on." He stroked my hair. "You want to give it another go?"

"Are you serious?"

"We're both single. I'm lonely, and you need to stop dating guys that treat you like crap. You aren't fooling me, either, Remy. I saw those bruises. Somebody knocked you around."

Okay, so Bjorn got a little insistent when he started pestering me to join him in the lifestyle.

My silence was answer enough.

"Let me protect you, Remy," he said. "I forgot—I forgot how nice it feels to be needed." He put his other arm around me. The warm embrace wriggled into my very core. Comforting. Safe. I rarely felt safe.

"Okay."

"Okay?" His voice sounded hopeful.

"Yeah, let's try again."

He hugged me tighter for a moment. "Let's get out of here. Where do you want to go?"

"I don't care."

"My place then." He pulled me to my feet. "We'll talk. Eat breakfast. I'll make eggs."

I found myself smiling. "That sounds great." We left the mess behind, and an idea started to form in my mind.

Cormac owed me a boon—I thought I knew what I would ask for. Looking at Ian, I felt that long buried love start to rustle and crack free of its shell.

This night hadn't turned out so bad after all.

As we headed for the door, Ian paused. "Your boon, we can't forget it."

"Cormac is gone."

"He left it on the throne. Come along." He led me to the throne I hadn't noticed earlier. It looked like a living thing and likely was. A flowering magnolia grown into a throne. It smelled like summer and sunshine.

Resting on one arm of the throne was an unremarkable stone. A flat, gray river rock imbued with Cormac's power. It hummed slightly.

"Only the intended recipient can pick it up."

I nodded and picked up the stone. It was cool to the touch, but I could feel its power in the vibration of its hum.

"Amazing." I breathed. "And it grants one wish?"

"Anything within the king's power," Ian replied.

In my hand was something more valuable than gold. I could ask for anything.

Cormac was sneaky, though, and his contracts notoriously tight. You had to come at them sideways.

I looked at Ian. "What I want is something Cormac won't give." Something I'd wanted twenty years ago.

Ian smiled. "I thank you for the thought."

"Cormac is a clever bastard, but he's no fox," I said. I gripped the stone tight. I couldn't break Cormac's hold on Ian, but I could loosen it. I could protect Ian against his influence.

"I wish for a touch of the true Blarney stone—in this stone."

The stone glowed for a moment, and I tossed it to Ian, who caught it reflexively. The stone turned to dust in his hand, the dust swirling and enveloping him in a green sparkling.

Ian's eyes went wide as the gift enveloped him. The true Blarney stone made a man immune to fey influence, able to lie without detection, and charismatic beyond human range. Its power would give Ian a longer leash.

"Oh, Remy." He smiled, a real proper smile. "I suppose foxes are immune to the Blarney stone?"

I grinned. "We are naturally consummate liars."

He stepped close to me and drew me into a kiss. "Let's go. Before you do anything else that makes me want to strip off all of your clothes."

I managed a bark of laughter. "That sounds like a wonderful prelude to breakfast."

"You are so easy to please." He kissed me again and took my arm in his. "You want bacon with the eggs?"

"Pancakes?"

"Waffles," he returned.

I smiled. "Waffles." We walked out of the ballroom, stepping over the scattered masks and detritus of the evening. We picked up my saxophone, and I realized my headache was gone, my anger about Bjorn had vanished. Soft music trembled through my veins. Happy music.

The melody added a bounce to my step, and we left the Hilton behind on foot. We walked two blocks to a posh apartment complex Cormac surely paid for. We headed inside, Ian nodding to the doorman—oh wow, a real doorman—and straight past the lobby guard. We took the elevator up to the fourth floor, and I tapped my foot against the beat of the elevator music.

"You never stop do you?" Ian remarked.

"Stop what?"

"Tapping your foot to the music."

"No, I guess I don't."

"It's cute."

"Great. You know, I get all sorts of adjectives. Cute, adorable, darling, sweet, but you know, no one has every once called me handsome," I remarked wryly.

"There's nothing wrong with being adorable. I've never been called adorable. Even as a child. My father thought it wasn't masculine."

"Poor Ian." I furrowed my eyebrows and gave him a kiss—I had to get on my toes to do it. "I think you're adorable."

"Thanks, Remy." He made a strange face and then picked me up, saxophone case and all, as the elevator doors opened.

"Hey, what the hell?"

"It's easier to kiss you like this," he replied, kissing me to prove his point. "Don't squirm."

"You put me down or I'll shift and we'll see how you like holding onto a wild fox."

"A wild fox stuck inside a suit? I think I could handle that." His voice was light. "It might even be cute."

He carried me out of the elevator and into a nearby apartment without fumbling his keys once. His apartment was fairly Spartan given how plush the complex was. There was a couch in the living room and a coffee table. The apartment was large. Really large. My apartment was a closet compared to this place.

On the coffee table was an album. I knew it was full of old photos of Ian's family.

He set me down on the couch. "I'll make breakfast."

I grabbed on to his tie and jerked him down onto the couch with me. "Breakfast can wait." I kissed him, a low growl escaping my throat.

Best. Samhain. Ever.

Believe Me, Beloved
by Charlie Cochet

Chapter 1

This was really happening.

Standing under the arched entrance to the grand ballroom, Robert Bradley was unable to do anything more than gape in absolute awe at the magnificence before him. Never in all his life had he seen such beauty and decadence. There was little around him that didn't gleam or sparkle, and if there truly was a financial crisis going on in the world, it certainly hadn't reached the walls of Gabriel Chase's colossal manor.

It was as if he had stepped through a magical gateway into another world, just like in his dime novels. However, unlike the men in his stories, no one would mistake Robert for a dashing hero. So much so, that as he stood, enraptured by the spectacle before him, he had no idea what to do with himself. In the last ten minutes alone, he had considered fleeing several times.

This world was so far removed from his own that it had him doubting the wisdom of accepting such an invitation. The top hat and tails he wore weren't even his own. They had been borrowed from the generous Mr. Dressler, who had not only supplied him with the invite in the first place, but had insisted he attend. Robert didn't even own the white tie and gloves he was sporting or the shined black shoes on his feet. He was a sham, an insignificant little imposter amongst a crowd of high-society elites for whom this ball was merely one of many in a string of seasonal diversions.

No matter how slick his hair, how straight his posture, he could never be one of them. The cost of one champagne glass alone was probably more than a month's rent on his little apartment, which would be a mere speckle of dust in this palace of rose marble and antique statuary. The walls and ceilings were heavily gilded, though he was hardly knowledgeable enough on the subject to know what period it was, and he prayed no one decided to talk to him concerning the topic. All he knew was that it was old and expensive, very expensive. Especially the three crystal chandeliers that hung from the ballroom ceiling, glittering like clusters of dazzling stars. There was one thing he was certain of. It was breathtaking.

From one end of the room, the white tuxedoed orchestra played a sweeping waltz for the hundreds of masked guests, most of who were dancing gracefully in the latest cut suits and most elegant of ball gowns. It was like a dream, and somewhere in that dream, *he* would be there. No doubt looking every bit the rugged Hollywood movie star people mistook him for.

What am I doing here? he asked himself yet again. Not even the mask concealing a portion of his face would be enough to hide his restless state. The fact that people were starting to notice him certainly wasn't helping his situation any, either.

He had been extremely relieved when Mr. Dressler had informed him he would be happy to provide a mask. After all, he had plenty, and even insisted that Robert keep it as a souvenir of the evening. Even the most simple of masks found at this ball would have been well out of Robert's price range.

At the moment, however, he wasn't feeling so relieved. He was the only one in the ballroom with a white mask. A great number of the guests wore red masks of various designs, some with large amounts of sparkling jewels and feathers. Odd, considering this was a black and white ball. Their masks also covered their whole faces. The rest of the guests wore either silver or gold more traditional masks that covered only a portion, like Robert's. He had started to ask Dressler why that was when the man had excused himself and run off. By then, Robert had become distracted by the object's exquisiteness. It almost appeared as if it was made of old marble, like some Greek artifact. It had tiny jewels and pearls set in the intricate, raised design of swirls. To each side of the mask was a white Pegasus. Both winged horses faced each other and between them, in the center of his brow, some kind of harp with a heart-shaped jewel in the center. It was truly beautiful. *Too beautiful,* he thought with a frown.

"Oh for crying out loud, Robert," he huffed under his breath. "Quit being such a coward." This was his chance. He should be grateful for it. He couldn't work in the mail room at Midnight Radio all his life. If he was going to show Mr. Chase what he was made of, now was the time. There was nothing he wanted more than the opportunity to sing on the radio. Well, there was perhaps one thing he wanted more, but that desire was unattainable.

Taking a deep, fortifying breath, Robert ignored all the stares he was getting as he made his way over to a waiter and, with a pleasant "thank you", took a glass of champagne. It might help settle his nerves some. Was it the mask or something else? He bit his bottom lip, and turning casually toward the wall, he discreetly checked himself. Everything seemed to be where it should be.

"Robert. So glad you could make it."

The boisterous greeting and hearty pat on the back

had him nearly jumping out of his skin, and he came dangerously close to dropping his champagne.

"Mr. Dressler." Robert quickly handed his champagne glass to a passing waiter in an attempt to save face before turning back to Dressler. "Thank you again so much for this opportunity and everything else you've done. You've been exceedingly generous. I hope you didn't go to too much trouble."

The tall, debonair blond waved a hand dismissively and smoothed a finger over his pencil-thin mustache. "No trouble at all. You're a very talented fellow. It's time for Gabriel Chase to see that."

Robert had to admit, when Dressler had approached him with the invitation, he had no idea what to make of it. The man had never so much as greeted him in the five years Robert had been working at Midnight Radio, and suddenly there he was with a personal invitation for Gabriel Chase's Black and White Ball. Not to mention the offer of a tuxedo, top hat, mask, and a list of reasons why he should sing for Mr. Chase. Had it been anyone else at Midnight, perhaps Robert wouldn't have been so stunned, but Dressler wasn't just anyone.

"I still don't understand why you chose me." Robert's cheeks flushed as he realized how rude that sounded. "What I mean is, I'm just a mailroom clerk, and you're *the* Arnold Dressler. You sang for Mr. Roosevelt just last year!"

"Yes, I did sing for Mr. Roosevelt," Dressler said with a chuckle. "I was also a newspaper boy once, too. Now look where I am." His piercing blue eyes pinned Robert to the spot. They were exceptionally pale in color and something about them—about Dressler himself—always made Robert feel a little unnerved, which of course then made him feel guilty. Dressler had never given him any reason to feel that way.

Dressler surprised Robert by putting an arm around his shoulders, turning him, and walking him toward the other end of the room where a number of majestic doors opened out to the gardens.

"Robert, I shall make a confession," Dressler said in a low voice. "I've heard you sing several times."

"You have?" Well, that was certainly news to him. Few people paid attention to the somewhat screwy mailroom clerk who went about singing to himself.

"Yes. I was waiting for my transcript when I overheard some of the girls talking about this amazing young man in the mailroom who had the most beautiful voice. Well, I simply had to hear for myself."

Robert listened to Dressler as they walked out onto the stone balcony. The moment he stepped foot outside and the cool night breeze swept through his hair, he found himself smiling. It was no surprise that the gardens were just as magnificent as the rest of the house. They stretched on for miles and were surrounded by forest. Everything was in full bloom, and there was an impressive array of flowers and statues painstakingly arranged about the grounds. More impressive, however, was the elaborate maze he could see at the far end. As they headed toward it, he marveled at the hedges trimmed into various animal shapes, everything from a life-sized elephant to a gathering of small rabbits. Above them, scores of glowing lanterns lit their path, and intertwined with all the foliage were stone pathways, each one curving and spiraling. Bubbling water features were strategically placed, creating an enchanting and magical feel.

"Beautiful, isn't it?" Dressler asked, snapping Robert out of his trance.

"I'll say. I've never seen anything like it. I was surprised to know Mr. Chase lived all the way out here. I thought he lived in Manhattan." The trip had cost him a pretty penny, having to take all those trains and taxis, but it was worth it to see all this.

"Oh, he has an apartment in the city of, course, but he's one of those odd birds who enjoys the countryside. He escapes here regularly," Dressler informed him, hand coming to rest on Robert's lower back as Dressler ushered him down the steps. Robert couldn't help wonder if it was deliberate. They walked farther down the grounds where he noticed there were fewer guests. He gave himself a good dressing down for being so silly. Dressler was merely being friendly.

"Would you like to see the maze?" Dressler asked.

Before Robert had a chance to speak up, he heard a familiar voice call out. "Arnold! Your brothers have been driving me mad asking for your whereabouts. Would you please go find them before they start harassing the rest of my guests?"

Robert froze, doing his damnedest not to show any signs of how the man's husky voice affected him.

"Yes, fine," Dressler grumbled and turned to Robert with a small bow. "Don't wander far. I shall return shortly."

Unable to speak, Robert simply nodded. Then he was alone. With *him*.

How much time had he spent daydreaming about those powerful shoulders, that strong jaw, and muscular chest? Not only was Gabriel Chase one of the most handsome, sought after bachelors in all of Manhattan, he was also Robert's boss. More troubling was the fact that he was the object of Robert's fantasies. It was of no help at all that the man possessed an uncanny resemblance to Mr. Gary Cooper. Robert had yet to miss a motion picture with the handsome film star.

Those brief moments when Robert happened to be walking the same hall as Gabriel always made his day, and then of course the images of coal-black hair and amber-colored eyes carried him through the nights. Even if Gabriel's mask had covered the whole of his face rather than merely his eyes, as it did now, Robert still would have recognized him. Though he had to admit, the scarlet red of the intricate piece combined with the intensity of those eyes was somewhat... hypnotizing.

"Oh, my apologies," Gabriel said with a polite bow. "I didn't realize Arnold was in the middle of a conversation." He tilted his head to one side and smiled, pointing to Robert's mask. "That's quite a unique one."

"It was a gift from Mr. Dressler," Robert replied, touching the mask somewhat self-consciously. "I hope you don't mind. I know it doesn't really match the others."

"A unique mask for a unique man, perhaps?"

His head snapped up at that, and he was surprised to find that Gabriel had closed the distance between them. Robert stood motionless, his gaze fixed on the amber eyes that appeared as if they were glowing. Gabriel had at least four inches on Robert's five feet ten, but his presence was far more imposing, giving him the impression of a much bigger man.

"You have beautiful eyes," Gabriel said. "Like the ocean. I love to swim in the ocean. Would you care to dance?"

Robert's heart nearly jumped out of his chest. "I beg your pardon?"

"Would you care to dance," Gabriel repeated.

Was the man mad? Certainly, this was his home, but it was filled with hundreds of guests. If anyone saw them, they would be ruined. There was always the chance that Gabriel might be able to use his money and influence to save himself from the workhouse or any charges of indecency, but Robert couldn't hope to be so lucky. Just the thought had him recoiling.

"You can't be serious."

Cursing himself for not having the good sense to at least reject the man civilly—no matter how hard his heart was fighting him on it—he half expected Gabriel to get angry and throw him out. Instead, the man let out a throaty laugh and pulled Robert into his arms.

"No one knows who you are," Gabriel assured him.

"But that's not true at all," Robert whispered hoarsely as he tried to pull away discreetly. "Mr. Dressler knows who I am. Everyone knows who *you* are."

"No one is going to say a thing. I promise you."

Robert wasn't so sure of that, but even as his entire body went on alert, he allowed Gabriel to lead him in a waltz, all the while wondering if the madness was spreading.

Chapter 2

"There are people watching," the young man murmured, his head lowered.

"No one here will say a word, sweetheart. I promise you." Gabriel knew that to be a fact. Most everyone here had a far more dangerous secret to keep, one that would keep any man or woman from revealing Gabriel's queerness to the outside world. Those who didn't possess the secret—the ones looking shocked and appalled—wouldn't be telling tales.

He pulled the young man closer, almost reluctant to think about what was to become of him. It was rare to find one who could so easily pass for innocent. What dastardly deed could this little morsel have performed? Leaning in, he took the young man's earlobe between his teeth and sucked it into his mouth, drawing the loveliest gasp from his dancing partner. He knew Dressler had claimed this one for his own, but Gabriel was feeling awfully tempted to steal the young man for himself. His scent was strong and riveting.

"You taste absolutely delicious." His arm tightened around the young man's slender waist, while his free hand roamed, caressing and exploring. Gabriel soon found himself fighting his baser instincts, and he inhaled deeply, fueling his growing lust. Suddenly, something familiar invaded his senses, and he stopped dead cold. He knew that scent. Please, God, don't let it be.

"Robert?"

"You know my name?" The young man pushed his mask up, revealing a beautiful face, one that Gabriel had made love to in his dreams for what seemed like an eternity.

"Of course I do," Gabriel snapped, moving the mask back down into place. He would know Robert's scent anywhere. All his time and effort spent resisting this particular temptation, only to have it land in his arms. Damn it all. "Why wouldn't I?"

"Well, it's a very big station, and with you being so important, I would hardly expect you to remember the name of one mailroom clerk," Robert replied bashfully.

"Never mind. What the hell are you doing here?" He hated the crushed look on Robert's face, but it was for his own good. Gabriel knew how careful Robert was, always making certain that when he looked at Gabriel, no one was watching. But Gabriel didn't need to catch those looks. He could smell the desire emanating from the young man's every pore. At times it had been pure torture just walking by him in the halls.

"I was invited." Robert's voice was quiet as he fidgeted, absently tugging at one end of his coat.

"Not by me you weren't." With a deep frown, he swatted Robert's hand away. "Stop that. You'll draw attention to yourself."

"I'm sorry. I didn't mean to..." Ocean-colored eyes became glassy, and Gabriel balled his fists at his sides. He knew he was being a complete ogre, but the mere thought that Robert had been deliberately placed in this situation by someone of his acquaintance was enough to get his blood boiling.

"Forgive me," Robert said, standing a little straighter and looking up at Gabriel, those eyes calling to him. "I didn't mean to cause any trouble. Am I...am I fired?"

"What?" Gabriel was surprised by that. Just what kind of man did Robert think he was? Well, considering his current behavior, he couldn't fault Robert for jumping to such a conclusion. "No. Don't be ridiculous."

With a nod, Robert took a step back, his gaze going to

the house. "I suppose I should go then."

"Why did you come?" Why was he asking? This was his opportunity to send Robert on his way, to fix things before they could get any worse. Yet, even knowing what he did, he was reluctant to let Robert go. What would become of them? What the hell was he talking about? There was no "them", and it was better off that way, for both of them.

Robert fidgeted again. When he realized he was pulling on his coat, he stopped, a lovely blush crawling up his neck and cheeks. "I was hoping I could...sing for you."

"You wanted to sing for me?" The thought shouldn't make him feel so goddamn happy, but it did, and he was having a great deal of trouble keeping the dopey grin off his face. He fought himself regardless. It would only give Robert hope. Gabriel had heard from several employees at the station of Robert's beautiful voice, but his concern for Robert's safety always won out, so he maintained his distance. He had even been considering putting in a good word for Robert at another station. Coward that he was, he kept putting it off.

"Yes. Well, I was hoping that perhaps you might let me audition for a spot on one of the programs. I'll start anywhere. I'll even do the sponsors."

Gabriel grabbed Robert's wrist and started for the house. "We have to get you out of here before--" He stopped in his tracks at the sight of Dressler and his brothers heading straight for them. It couldn't be too late. He wouldn't allow it. Spinning Robert, Gabriel pushed him forward. "Move, quickly."

"Is something wrong? Where are we going?" Robert asked worriedly, glancing over his shoulder at him.

"No time to explain, just walk." The scent in the air changed, forcing Gabriel to grab Robert's arm and break into a run. "Run! As fast as you can!" To his relief,

Robert didn't ask questions, simply attempted to keep up with him as he sprinted through the garden with Robert in tow. They had almost reached the end when the wolves descended.

"Oh my God!" Robert gasped. "Where did those dogs come from? Wait, those dogs look an awful lot like--" His eyes widened, and he turned to Gabriel. "What the hell are wolves doing in your garden?"

"Going somewhere, my dear friend?" Dressler asked, his loathing for Robert very evident in his eyes. Poor Robert looked utterly stunned and confused. Gabriel wished he could set his mind at ease, but he couldn't afford to take his eyes off Dressler.

"You son-of-a-bitch," Gabriel spat out. "How dare you bring him here! He's an innocent." He knew Dressler hadn't been happy with him for a good while now, but to do this? It was unacceptable and in blatant violation of the code.

Dressler scoffed at that. "No human is innocent. Their mere existence is a crime against nature."

"It's against the rules," Gabriel reminded Dressler heatedly.

"And we're growing quite weary of your rules, Gabriel. Times have changed. The scales have tipped in favor of greed and corruption. Oversaturation. Now, the innocent...*there* is a sport worth pursuing. There are far fewer of those about. Imagine what the old dogs would be willing to pay for one of them? I can understand your hesitation. He is rather lovely to look at, and I imagine even lovelier to bed. I would have been able to confirm the latter if you hadn't interrupted us." He cast a Gabriel a wicked look. "He's a virgin."

Gabriel's head snapped in Robert's direction. "Really? But you're nearly twenty-five!"

Heat flared up Robert's face. "Well, one can't be too

careful these days, and it's not as if I have no experience at all. I've done things, just not…you know." He cleared his throat and crossed his arms over his chest. "I don't have to explain my actions to you. Who I have in my bed, and when, is of no consequence to anyone."

Walking calmly up to Robert, Dressler took Robert's chin in his gloved hand. "Perhaps we might be able to come to an agreement. For old time's sake. What do you say, Gabriel? Share and share alike?"

Chapter 3

Robert smacked Dressler's hand away from him and spoke through clenched teeth. "Put your hands on me again and I guarantee you a bloodied nose."

Just because he lacked experience in certain areas, hardly meant he was about to stand for this appalling display. He turned to Gabriel and shook his head, his heart heavy. "I never would have imagined such behavior from you." Removing his mask, he tossed it at Dressler's feet, along with his gloves. "I'll make certain the rest is delivered to you first thing in the morning."

How could he have been so wrong about Gabriel? Turning once more to the man who had occupied his thoughts and dreams for so long, Robert did his best not to let his disappointment show. "Is this what you do? Go to great lengths to humiliate poor saps like me?" He swallowed hard and ignored the pleading look in Gabriel's eyes. No doubt the man was feeling guilty for this tasteless prank now that it had backfired, but it was too late. Robert had seen his true colors.

"Well, I hope you both have a swell time laughing at my expense. Good evening, gentlemen." Robert turned to go when one of the large dogs materialized before him, snapping at him with a jaw full of razor-sharp teeth. Good God, it really *was* a wolf!

In his haste to get away, Robert lost his footing and landed on his rear. He stared up at the wolf, which seemed to have doubled in size, its pupils dilated and its teeth bare.

"Gabriel!" Robert cried out in a moment of panic as he scrambled back, the soles of his shoes slipping on the moist grass. His whole body was on alert, and a terrible sense of dread washed over him as the pack of wolves prowled toward him with Dressler at the head. It was almost as if they were following his lead. That was impossible.

Robert had never been more frightened in his life, and just when he thought things couldn't get any worse, something even more improbable happened. A strange, loud sound, resembling a deep, chesty cough, echoed in Robert's ear, and for a moment he feared he had breathed his last breath. He stared wide-eyed and in disbelief at the big, powerful, black cat that stepped over him.

Heaven almighty, now there were wild cats, too? What sort of place was this? Was there a zoo somewhere on the grounds that he had been unaware of? He didn't know which to be frightened of more, the wolves or the jaguar. Either way, Robert was about to become someone's dinner. He sat very still, afraid that if he moved, the jaguar would turn those frightful fangs on him. Why the thing hadn't devoured him already was beyond his comprehension. It had to weigh over two hundred pounds. More disconcerting was the fact that Dressler didn't appear concerned in the least. In fact, he looked...smug.

Robert tried to spot Gabriel from the corner of his eye, praying the man was all right. He was stunned to find him gone. Had Gabriel just run off and left him there to die?

"Gabriel..." The word left his lips in a whisper, and the large, sleek cat turned its head. It stared straight at him. "Oh my God." Those eyes... "It's not possible." Robert shook his head, refusing to believe the insanity of what was transpiring before him. He had to be losing his mind. There was no way...

"You can't protect him, Gabriel," Dressler stated as he calmly pulled at his gloves one finger at a time, as if he was merely having a discussion about the weather over coffee. "It's far too late for that. You should have stolen him away from me and left your mark on him sooner. I gave you ample opportunity."

To Robert's utter astonishment, the large cat's head slightly lowered, and a grunt-like sound escaped.

"Yes, I imagine you are feeling rather foolish now, aren't you? You think I didn't notice your effort to stay away from him? Did you truly think that would stop us? Poor, naïve Gabriel." Dressler tsked.

Robert couldn't tear his gaze away from the black jaguar Dressler continued to address as Gabriel. He found himself compelled to ask, "What's going on?" He hated how shaky his voice sounded, but considering the circumstances, he believed he had every right to. Why was no one finding any of this even remotely disturbing? And why weren't there shrieks and shouts coming from panicking guests? When he looked over his shoulder, he discovered why. There were no guests. Everyone had cleared off.

Swell.

"The truth is more than your feeble little human mind could comprehend," Dressler replied haughtily, hitting Robert's last nerve. He narrowed his eyes and lifted his chin defiantly.

"Try me."

"The short of it is: we are not human. We are an evolved species. A melding of two souls, human and animal. Though some have a habit of attempting to suppress their more innate natures more than others, such as my dear friend here." Dressler cast the jaguar a reproachful look before shifting his gaze back to Robert. His eyes looked somewhat brighter than they had before. "This ball is a longstanding tradition, a means to satisfying that certain...itch. That is why your mask was different from the rest. So there could be no mistaking that I had claimed you for my own."

It suddenly dawned on Robert. "The different colors..."

"That's how we mark our prey. Provide each morsel with a distinctive mask of our design. Those donning gold and silver will not be leaving this ball. And neither shall you."

"You're going to hunt all those people?" Robert couldn't believe what he was hearing. Despite the sheer implausible yarn he had just been told, he couldn't keep himself from feeling sick to his stomach. "You're nothing but murderers."

That earned him a truly sinister laugh that sent an awful chill up his spine. "Actually, the murderers are in there," Dressler replied, pointing to the mansion. "And they wear silver and gold, dining on caviar and drinking champagne."

"What?" Robert asked, stunned.

"It was Gabriel's idea. Trés uninspiring, but the majority won the vote. I'm hardly about to get into the tedious task of explaining Gabriel's oh-so-grand family history, but the gist of it is that we are limited by our 'laws' into hunting those who have escaped persecution for their heinous crimes. It's all very carefully monitored. You'll find nothing but the most rotten in there." Dressler let out a heavy sigh. "Sadly, it somehow taints the meat. Gabriel may be content to give us spoils, but I have had enough, quite frankly." A big, toothy grin spread across Dressler's face. "Shall we start the fun? I will even give you a head start."

Before Robert's very eyes, in a series of chilling, gruesome twists and growls, Dressler ceased to be. In his place was a fair-haired wolf far larger and more terrifying than the other three grays behind him. If Robert hadn't seen it with his own eyes, he would never have believed it. He sat, stupefied, until the jaguar turned its head and bumped it against Robert's chest.

"Gabriel? Is...is it really you?" he asked, feeling like a complete pill, talking to a two hundred pound predator as if it was some common house cat.

A purr that sounded a great deal like a small chainsaw reverberated from the massive beast as he rubbed his head against the side of Robert's. Shutting his eyes tight, Robert braced himself. Instead of receiving a deadly bite, he received a rather broad lick up his cheek.

"Um, please, don't do that," Robert muttered and opened his eyes to find the jaguar watching him. "I don't mean to offend, it just feels...incredibly odd."

There was a fierce growl from Dressler, and some unspoken exchange seemed to go on between him and Gabriel. One that resulted in Gabriel pushing his head into Robert's chest and making strange sounds.

"You can't be serious. Don't tell me you want me to run?" Robert asked him. Even with the knowledge that it was Gabriel, when the jaws opened and ferocious roar came out, Robert was on his feet and making tracks across the gardens.

"This can't be happening. This can't be happening," he chanted over and over as he ran past statues and water features, kicking up grass and gravel as he did. Where the hell was he supposed to go? This damn place was like Central Park and most of it was just as badly lit. "This is impossible." The odds against him were staggering. Dressler and his pack could surely smell him from miles away, not to mention could see far better in the dark than he could. If he didn't get pounced on and eaten, he would probably end up running head first into a tree!

Once he had made it inside the forest, which may or may not have been the worst possible idea, he found himself in a thicket that looked the same from every direction. All he had wanted to do was sing on the radio. Was that so wrong? Was it worth being hunted like some quail or rabbit? He wasn't even going to get into the fact that the man of his dreams was some human, animal, beast-like creature. He should have stayed in Jersey.

A huge lump of shadow sprung out from his right, and he couldn't hold back his yelp. Despite it being Gabriel, Robert ran in the opposite direction. A few more feet into the thicket, and Gabriel sprung out again, this time ahead of him. With a frustrated grunt, Robert turned and took another route, all the while wondering where Dressler was. Not that he was keen to see the man—uh wolf—but that could only mean he was up to something.

Making it out of the shrubbery, he found himself directly opposite the maze's entrance, though he had to run across a somewhat expansive clearing to make it there. Again, Gabriel sprung out, and Robert clutched at his chest.

"Oh for the love of God! Will you please stop popping out of bushes? You're going to give me a heart attack!" When Gabriel pushed his head against the back of Robert's legs, he realized the jaguar had been herding him, getting him to turn where he had wanted. It was a rather farfetched notion, but no more than everything else that had transpired up until now. Had Gabriel been keeping Dressler from him, too?

Gabriel kept pushing, and Robert spun around, holding his hands out in front of him. "Now just hold on a minute. If I go in there, there will be no way out. I'll be trapped." He stood still as Gabriel walked around him, rubbing his head against Robert's legs and giving him little pushes. "Fine. You better know what you're on about," Robert grumbled, absently scratching the cat's head and receiving another of those chainsaw-like purrs. It was only when he removed his hand that he noticed the blood on it. "You're bleeding!"

There was no time for further inspection as two of the wolves emerged from the trees. Cursing under his breath, Robert made a dash for the maze. He had almost made it when he collided with something hard and heavy. He was thrown to the ground, and the wind was knocked out of him. He threw his arm up, expecting it to be shredded to pieces, when a piercing yelp escaped the sharp-toothed canine. Its head was now in Gabriel's jaw, and he dragged the wolf off Robert as if it didn't weigh a thing. To Robert's astonishment, the wolf was still alive. Gabriel hadn't killed it. More surprising was the fact that the other wolf had stopped in its tracks, lowering himself closer to the ground with his ears drawn back as he made a whimpering sound. It was somewhat of a relief to know the brothers cared about each other more than they did sinking their teeth into Robert.

Not waiting around for Dressler to make an appearance, Robert took off into the maze just as Gabriel had wanted him to. Behind him was a horrible cacophony of roars, growls, and yelps. He wished he could do Gabriel proud by trying to find his own way, but the hedges were at least twelve feet high and he had never been in here before. How could he possibly know which way to turn?

As soon as he felt the nudge at the back of his legs, he realized he didn't have to. This time, Gabriel went ahead of him, and Robert ran as fast as he could to keep up, all the while wondering how far off Dressler and his pack were. In no time, they were at the center of the maze. It was square, with a stone bench on each side, and potted roses. In the center was an old, large, stone, two-tiered water fountain that was empty. There was also no way out.

"Damn it, what now?" Robert asked Gabriel, allowing the large cat to push him toward the fountain. He put his hands on the old chipped stone and arched an eyebrow at his feline companion. "And what am I supposed to do? Climb in and hope for the best?" Gabriel continued to push him against the fountain. "You can't be serious?"

In one graceful bound, Gabriel was inside the large bowl, and he pawed at the edge. Good God, he actually wanted Robert to climb in.

"This is sheer madness," Robert grumbled as he climbed in. "All right. Now what, Mr. Smart Guy?"

Gabriel pawed at the base of the centerpiece in one specific spot. Taking a closer look, Robert noticed one of the stone flowers was slightly off kilter. Pushing on it with all his strength, he was stunned when the stone shifted, revealing a hole that was big enough for him to fit through and a set of stairs. "Incredible," he breathed and quickly started to descend. As soon as he was in, Gabriel followed. Climbing back up, he looked around the opening and just inside found an exact copy of the flower he had pushed to get it. In no time the stone moved back into place, and he was plunged into complete darkness.

A lamp suddenly sprang to life, its gold flame casting a warm glow about the place. Turning, he gasped at the sight before him.

"Gabriel!" Robert swiftly climbed down the steps and ran to him, catching the larger man just as his knees gave out beneath him. Doing his best to keep Gabriel from hitting the floor, Robert spotted a bed at the end of the room, and putting one of Gabriel's arms around his shoulder, he walked the man over. Carefully, he helped Gabriel down onto the soft mattress, and by the time he had removed Gabriel's shoes and lifted his legs onto the bed, the man was out for the count.

Looking around, Robert realized the place was made up to be some sort of makeshift, underground apartment, complete with small kitchen and water pump. Why on earth would anyone need such a place? Then again, he should thank his lucky stars it was here. There was a low groan, drawing his attention. Robert had been so concerned with the danger they had been in, he hadn't noticed how bad a shape Gabriel was in.

"What have they done to you?" he asked softly, taking in Gabriel's bloodied state. His shirt had been all but torn to shreds, and his pants weren't that much better off. He had bites and slashes all over his body; so many that Robert couldn't begin to guess which ones all the blood belonged to. He went quickly around the room, gathering what supplies he could find, and gave a little prayer of thanks when he came across a first aid kit. Whatever this place was, it was well equipped.

With all the tenderness he possessed, he got to work cleaning Gabriel's wounds. As he did, he was surprised to find they weren't nearly as deep as they had first appeared to be. When he took a closer look, he received another revelation. The wounds were healing unnaturally quickly. Putting such thoughts aside, he finished attending to Gabriel. Once he had, he pulled the blanket out very carefully from under Gabriel, and before he could talk himself out of it, he removed his shoes and climbed up onto the bed. He lay beside Gabriel and pulled the covers over them.

As he lay on his side facing Gabriel, his head buzzing with endless questions and even more concerns, he found himself unable to take his eyes off the man's rugged face. Everything he thought he had known about Gabriel meant nothing now. Yet, as his fingers lightly stroked the man's face, he couldn't help but feel his heart swell. He had no idea what to make of Gabriel Chase, of what he was and what he did, but Robert's heart simply refused to listen to reason. With his hand over Gabriel's heart, he soon drifted to sleep.

Chapter 4

What the hell was going on? Where was he?

The moment that sweet musk filled his lungs, Gabriel remembered everything. His eyes flew open, and he bolted upright, his muscles tense and ready for action. There was nothing. Nothing but the faint, soft snores of the very heavenly figure lying beside him.

Gabriel took a moment to just sit there and watch Robert sleep. In his many, many years of living this life, he had never come across a creature he desired more than the one before him. He didn't know what it was about Robert that made him feel as such. There was really nothing all that extraordinary about the tawny-haired young man. He was lovely to look at, yes, but so were many others, many even lovelier. Robert was shy, somewhat uncoordinated, and more often than not, quite uncertain of himself. He was a tad on the slender side, which gave the impression that he was younger than he was, but Gabriel knew that was only because the silly boy had a habit of spending his grocery money on music sheets too often. He had become so concerned for the man, he had been forced to provide free lunch for his employees, just so he knew that Robert would at least be eating one proper meal a day.

Robert was certainly infuriating at times, with the oddest quirks. Like always missing a spot when he shaved, usually somewhere on his neck. If Robert only knew how much Gabriel looked forward to discovering that spot on a daily basis, he would no doubt take extra care to make certain it never occurred, which was probably why Gabriel had never pointed it out to him. The young man was a puzzle indeed, and Gabriel had never been more riveted.

Tearing himself away, he carefully stood and went to the large trunk at the far end of the room where he had extra clothing. Placing a new pair of black pants, matching vest, tie, and a white shirt on the trunk's lid, he removed his ruined clothes and stood in his shorts. Stretching his arms high above his head and clasping his hands together, he felt his muscles pull. He was still a little sore, but at least his wounds had healed.

A soft gasp caught his ear, and he turned, surprised to see Robert awake and sitting up, his gaze fixed on Gabriel's chest. It was as if the air had been sucked out of the room, and the heat coming off both of them was enough to have Gabriel struggling against his more primitive side. Robert was human, something he could not allow himself to forget.

"I'm sorry if I woke you," Gabriel said, his voice coming out rougher than he had hoped. Robert's scent was playing havoc with his body. "Good God!" He threw his hands in front of him in a feeble attempt to hide his erection, the heat rushing to his face.

"It's all right," Robert assured him and patted the bed next to him.

"I don't think that would be wise," Gabriel murmured. If Robert had that kind of effect on him from this distance, who knew what would happen if he drew any closer. "I... fear I may not be able to control myself." If anything was going to happen between them, it would be on Robert's terms, and he would make certain the young man knew exactly what he was getting into. Despite how deep in this mess Robert already was.

"Oh." Robert nodded his understanding but stayed where he was, sitting in the middle of the bed. "Are they still out there?"

"Yes." At Robert's alarmed expression, Gabriel quickly elaborated. "But they don't know about this place. I made it years ago in case of such an emergency. They can't get to us down here." He tapped the side of his nose. "Smell, you see. Our scent may lead them here, but when you sealed the entrance, it triggered the fountain. The water contains a special mixture of mine and will destroy whatever scent was left behind."

"But we can't stay down here forever," Robert said, with a mixture of frustration and worry. "Are they going to kill me?"

"No," Gabriel growled, causing Robert to start. When he spoke again, he took on a gentler tone. "I won't let them."

Robert folded his arms on his drawn up knees and brought his chin down with a heavy sigh. "How are you going to stop them? There's five of them and one of you."

"I can dispatch Dressler's brothers," Gabriel replied confidently. "I'm stronger, have more muscle than them, and my claws are sharper. My bite is also far more powerful than theirs." Something in his face must have given him away, because a tender expression crossed Robert's.

"You don't want to kill them, do you?"

Gabriel shook his head and took a seat on the trunk beside his clothes. "I don't kill my own kind, even if they are complete bastards. Dressler's brothers aren't bad, really. They just have a terrible leader. None of them would dare oppose Dressler. I could dispatch him easily, but he is truly without shame. He would make his brothers step in if he felt he was about to be defeated."

"So, is there any way out?"

Gabriel nodded and shifted uncomfortably, wishing he could get dressed, but he was too embarrassed by his current state of arousal to move any more than he already had. Now came the more difficult part. He nodded toward the wooden door to his left. "That leads to the front driveway. I can get you there, take you to the docks and put you on the first ocean-liner to Europe. I have a house in the English countryside you could stay in and--"

Robert put a hand up, bringing him to a halt. "Out of the question. I am not going to let that fiend exile me from my own home. Nor am I about to live on your charity."

"It's not charity," Gabriel replied, feeling somewhat affronted. "I put you in this situation; therefore, I have every right to see you are taken care of."

"First of all, I am not your mistress. I have no need to be taken care of by anyone." Robert crossed his arms over his chest with a defiant pout. "You did not put me in this situation, Dressler did."

"But you'll be alive," Gabriel said, trying to talk some sense into Robert. If he were honest with himself, Gabriel would admit he rather liked the idea of taking care of the man. Blasted brat was stubborn.

"Not in my book." Robert shifted and came to sit on the edge of the bed, his head tilted to one side and his bright blue-green eyes peering at Gabriel. "There's another option isn't there? One you're reluctant to mention. I want to hear it."

Knowing Robert wouldn't rest until he had heard it all, Gabriel gave in. "I could make you my mate."

That certainly got Robert's attention, and his brows shot up. "Mate? As in…"

"Marking you and well…um, you know. Relieving you of your virginity."

"I see."

The room was very quiet for a very long time, enough to bring Gabriel out of his aroused state in exchange for an equally uncomfortable one. After what seemed like hours, but was surely only minutes, Robert looked over at him, his cheeks a bright red.

"So, what would 'marking' me entail?"

Gabriel gaped at Robert. "You can't be serious." He jumped to his feet and started pacing furiously. "You have no notion what it means, of how serious a situation you would find yourself in."

"Obviously if you don't explain it to me, I won't understand, will I?" Robert replied defensively.

"In the eyes of my society, we would be bound to each other. If you were to break that pact, I could no longer protect you, and no other of my kind would touch you because you would be considered ruined. They may even kill you to protect their secret or, at the very least, have you imprisoned. Mating is not something we take lightly."

"Oh?" Robert arched a brow at that. "Because before you knew who I was, you didn't seem too hesitant about mating."

"Sex and mating are not the same," Gabriel growled as he marched over and loomed over Robert, his fists on his hips. "We would be offering far more than our bodies, Robert. I have no intention of giving you my heart only to have you trample on it with your callous human nature."

"I beg your pardon?" Robert scrambled onto his feet, wobbling a little on the bed before standing to his full height, his arms crossed over his chest. "Now you listen here. If you think I'm going to be intimidated, you have another think coming. If this is going to work, then you have to stop thinking of me as the weaker species."

Gabriel opened his mouth for a rebuttal, then closed it. "Huh?"

"You heard me," Robert retorted, poking Gabriel in the shoulder. "If you think I'm going to let you treat me like the weaker species or like the little woman, you've got another think coming."

"But…" Gabriel shook his head, attempting to get his jumbled thoughts into some sort of order. When he couldn't, he looked up at Robert, who was smiling sweetly. He stepped up to Gabriel and slid his arms around Gabriel's neck. "Are you certain that's what you want?" Gabriel asked him.

Robert placed gentle kisses over Gabriel's face and slowly, sensually rubbed up against him. "I can't think of anyone else I would want myself bound to."

"You'll draw a great deal of attention from the society," Gabriel informed him, voice growing husky as his own arms wrapped around Robert's waist.

"I think I can handle it, as long as you're by my side. Will you stay by my side, Gabriel?"

"As long as you'll have me." He crushed his lips to Robert's, his need overwhelming. Robert tasted even better than in Gabriel's dreams, and he couldn't get enough. His tongue delved deep, exploring and plundering, demanding more and more from Robert. The heat coming from both their bodies, the mixture of scents and sounds coming from the man in his arms had him crawling onto the bed and pulling Robert down on top of him. They were a flurry of hands, and in no time, Gabriel had relieved Robert of his clothing.

Whatever Robert lacked in experience, he more than made up for in enthusiasm and sheer unrestrained lust. It took everything Gabriel had not to flip Robert over and have his way with the man. He kept reminding himself that this was Robert's first time, and as soon as Gabriel put himself in position, Robert's nerves would kick in. Whatever he might be feeling, however badly he wanted to lose himself, this was not about him. It was about Robert.

"Oils," Gabriel said against Robert's lips as hands roamed down his body and took hold of his shorts.

"What?"

"Get the oils." Gabriel pointed off toward the little makeshift kitchen. "Second drawer on the left." Robert started to protest, but Gabriel shook his head and gave Robert a gentle shove. "Please."

Bounding off the bed, Robert made a racket searching for the oils and, once he had them, ran back to bed. He handed the two small, glass bottles to Gabriel, who placed them on the bed. Then he grabbed Robert and pulled the man back down on him, attacking those delicious lips. Robert writhed and wriggled on top of him, his hands taking hold of Gabriel's member and bringing him to arch his back off the bed. He cursed under his breath and planted a fist against the old wooden headboard as Robert slid down his body and took him in his hot mouth.

"Oh Geez," Gabriel gasped, shutting his eyes tight and biting down on his bottom lip. Robert proceeded to display exactly how good he was at "other things", as Robert had put it. Gabriel had known Robert was a talented singer, but had no idea his talents extended to the bedroom.

Robert made little humming noises as he licked, sucked, and nipped at Gabriel. He went from taking the whole of Gabriel's shaft down to the root back up to just licking and toying with the tip. Before Gabriel knew it, he had to grab Robert's shoulder.

"Stop, stop!" He wasn't going to last another second like this. Pulling Robert to sit on his stomach, Gabriel grabbed one of the small bottles and poured some oil into his hand.

"Why are you on the bottom?" Robert asked, sitting astride Gabriel.

"Because I need you to take the lead."

"Why?"

"So I won't hurt you." With his free hand, Gabriel smacked Robert's bottom playfully. "Lean forward."

Robert's cheeks turned the most wonderful shade of pink, and he did as Gabriel asked. "You're not going to hurt me," he murmured.

Hushing his lover with a deep, passionate kiss, Gabriel reveled in the surprised gasp he received when he started pushing his finger inside Robert.

"Oh, my," Robert whispered through a shaky breath, wriggling around Gabriel's finger, his eyes shut tight.

"Are you all right?" Gabriel asked, receiving a little nod. "Robert, look at me." Opening his eyes, Robert met Gabriel's gaze. "We must always be honest with each other."

"Okay. I'm fine, it just feels... odd."

Gabriel smiled and gave Robert's lips a sweet kiss. "That's all right. Breathe deeply and try to relax. If it hurts or you change your mind, you tell me. Got it?"

"Yes."

It took some time, but Gabriel wasn't about to risk hurting Robert. He wanted Robert's first time—*their* first time—to be a good experience for his young lover. Reining in the beast inside him, he did everything he could to take things slow, always checking that Robert was all right. Soon, Robert was lowering himself onto Gabriel in the slowest, most excruciating way, but Gabriel clenched his teeth and gripped the edges of the bed while Robert paused and backtracked until Robert was finally settled on him. The tight heat surrounding him was the most glorious and painful thing he had ever experienced. Then Robert started moving, and Gabriel released a low, deep growl from inside his chest.

A wicked gleam came into Robert's gaze, his smile positively sinful as he picked up his pace. They were both soon panting, and Robert's fingers dug into the flesh of Gabriel's chest in the most delicious way. His own fingers dug into Robert's hips, but he did his best to remember himself.

"Oh, my," Robert repeated over and over, bringing

Gabriel to chuckle. "You think that's funny, do you?" Robert asked, trying to fight a smile and losing miserably. He leaned forward and impaled himself on Gabriel, bringing a string of curses from both of them.

"Damn the hell, what?" Gabriel knew that what he said made absolutely no sense, but his mind had ceased functioning, and as Robert threw his head back and rode Gabriel like a man possessed, all Gabriel could do was give himself over to his lover. Never in all his dreams of having Robert in his bed, had it been like this. Every muscle in his body was strained, his toes curling and pulse soaring. He felt his release drawing closer, and he tried to warn Robert, but instead all that came out was a jumble of sounds.

Unable to hold back anymore, he dug his fingers into Robert's hip until he had his lover's undivided attention. "Touch yourself," he ordered, taking over and thrusting into Robert repeatedly, deep and hard, drawing the most tantalizing gasps and moans from his lover.

Robert pleasured himself, his pace matching Gabriel's thrusts, and suddenly a blinding white light burst in front of his vision, drawing a growl from Gabriel as his release plowed into him. On his last thrust, Robert cried out, his semen coating Gabriel's chest in ribbons.

Collapsing onto Gabriel's chest, Robert wrapped his arms around Gabriel's neck and buried his face. For a moment, Gabriel panicked, wondering if he had ended up hurting Robert after all.

"Are you all right? Robert, talk to me," Gabriel managed between panting breaths.

Pulling slowly away, Robert gazed down at him lovingly. Robert was the most beautiful creature Gabriel had ever seen. He was sweaty, flushed, and positively glowing.

"I'm more than all right," Robert replied quietly

and proceeded to kiss him tenderly. For the next few hours, Robert showed Gabriel that he was indeed more than all right. He was also a quick learner.

Chapter 5

"Ready?"

Robert looked up at Gabriel and, with a smile he could barely contain, nodded. His whole body was on fire and would be aching for days to come, but he wouldn't trade it for anything in the world. He knew the commitment they were making was not to be taken lightly. There were a great many new experiences ahead for both of them, as well as a great deal of scandal from Gabriel's society. Although they were safe to express their affection to each other within the confines of the society, they would not be allowed such privilege from the outside world. It was something Gabriel was accustomed to, but not Robert. Even walking into the garden with his hand in Gabriel's had him feeling exceptionally nervous.

There was so much he would have to learn. He looked down at the bandage around his arm and the new scars he would soon have. Gabriel had made certain not to cut too deeply, but the four claw marks on his forearm still burned, and would do so for some time. He knew he probably should have found the whole thing rather disturbing, but being marked as Gabriel's felt...right.

"You son-of-a-bitch, what have you done?" Dressler and his now human pack appeared before them, and Gabriel pulled Robert behind him. "You mated with him?" the blond spat out.

"Yes, and marked him. You know what will happen to you if you touch him," Gabriel replied, holding his head up high.

"You bound yourself to a human just to spite me?" Dressler asked in disbelief.

Gabriel scoffed at that. "You think far too highly of

yourself, Arnold. I did it because I care for him."

"Your father is going to have kittens. Figuratively speaking of course," Dressler added with a fiendish grin. "Especially knowing that you have bound yourself to not merely a human, but one who cannot provide any heirs. I cannot wait until that tidbit of news spreads across society. It seems, in a way, I still win." He gave Robert a little bow and started to walk away, then paused. Turning, his eyes gleamed dangerously. "Come to think of it, this victory is not sufficient. Be warned Gabriel, this is not over. You will pay for your betrayal."

Without another word, Dressler and his pack were gone, and Robert was left wondering what was going on. There was more to all this than either man were letting on. As if reading his mind, Gabriel spoke up.

"It's a very old rivalry," Gabriel explained. "I've tried to put a stop to it many a time, to no avail. The only reason he hasn't taken matters further is because of my father."

"Who is...?" Robert prompted, not in the least bit encouraged by Gabriel's inability to look him in the eye. "Gabriel?"

"He's the head of the society," he replied with a sigh.

Robert went to cross his arms over his chest, and forgetting his wounds, let out a string of ungentlemanly curses when he inadvertently pressed down on them. Once the onslaught of cursing subsided, he turned to Gabriel, who most certainly should be cringing. "And you didn't think to mention this earlier?"

"I didn't think it was of any importance."

"Not of any--" Robert threw his arms up in frustration. "Unbelievable! Your father is the head of your society, who, by the way, is expecting you to provide heirs, and you didn't think it was of any importance? Oh my God," he gasped. "He's going to eat me, isn't he?"

Gabriel stared at him, then burst into laughter. With a glare, Robert started marching off.

"I'm sorry, please forgive me," Gabriel pleaded, catching up with Robert and pulling him into strong arms. "I would be lying if I said he won't be upset or disappointed, but I truly do care for you, Robert. I've been dreaming of having you in my arms for five years, and now that I have you, I have no intention of giving you up. Not for my father, Dressler, or anyone. Please. I'm going to need you by my side."

Robert knew it was futile. He couldn't deny Gabriel. The truth of the matter was that he didn't want to give Gabriel up, either, nor did he want to give up the opportunity of a future with the man.

"Do I still get to sing for you?" he asked as they walked together toward the unknown.

"You mean more than you did when we were making love?" Gabriel teased.

Robert gave him a playful shove. "You pill! I'm bound to an uncouth beast."

With the most wonderful laugh, Gabriel pulled Robert close and kissed him.

Robert had no notion what was in store for him, and he was quite certain it wouldn't be easy. There was so much they still had to talk about, such as the troubling traditions of Gabriel's society, but Robert had spent so long keeping himself safe, afraid to take any risks, that he had almost missed his greatest opportunity, a chance at happiness. Taking Gabriel's hand, Robert kissed his cheek and started toward the mansion. Whatever awaited them, they would face it together.

Masks Off!

As You Wish
By Rob Rosen

It took me hours to reach the castle, my meager belongings slung over my shoulder, eyes wide as the massive stone structure came into view. It sat deep within the forest, the trees ancient, moss hanging down like beards off impossibly thick branches. My heart thumped madly inside my chest as I approached, a trickle of sweat sliding down my forehead before stinging my eyes. I would've turned and run, but I desperately needed the position, the money, times being what they were.

I paused when I approached the wooden door, my hand coming to rest on the brass knocker, a white-hot chill suddenly riding down my back. Still, I lifted it up and sent it clanging. *Boom, boom, boom* it went, the sound resonating from behind the door, echoing in my chest.

I waited, listening for footsteps from within. My leg bounced nervously as I slicked my hair back and straightened my jacket. First impressions were all I had. And the walk back would be a long one if the meeting went poorly.

The door eventually creaked open. The lord of the manor answered, surprising me to the quick. He was tall, taller than me by far, thin in an athletic sort of way, impeccably dressed in silk and cotton, all in various shads of gray and purple, and a face I'd only ever seen before in my dreams. Impossibly handsome, he was, hair long and cascading over his shoulders, a perfectly trimmed goatee sprouting from his chin, aquiline nose, full lips, and eyes the color of the sky on a hot summer's day. Eyes so blue you could practically take a swim in them.

He smiled radiantly when he saw me, my heart once again pounding. "James," he said, his voice deep and resonating.

I nodded and forced a smile in return. "Your highness," I replied with a slight bow.

He stared at me and then broke out into a fit of laughter. "Merely a duke," he managed through a coughing fit as tears streamed down his cheeks. "Save the *your highness* for the king."

"The king?" I croaked out.

He shrugged. "You'll meet him eventually, I suppose." He wiped the tears away and further opened the door. "And, please, call me Charles," he added, motioning me inside.

And so I followed him in, the door slamming loudly behind us. I held out my hand. "A pleasure, Charles," I managed.

His smile returned, his hand held out before it grasped my own, flesh on flesh, my body suddenly on fire as our eyes met, locked. "That it is, James," he said, voice thick as molasses and equally as sweet. "That it is."

I stood there, gazing at him, and him at me, hand in hand, the hair on the back of my neck standing on end. "So, um, shall we begin the interview?" I asked, reluctantly releasing his grip from my own.

He moved farther inside, past the foyer and into an enormous living room, the fire ablaze, furnishings beyond rich. "You've already come recommended," he said, sitting on a couch as I took a seat on a nearby chair. "The position is yours, if you'll have it."

I sat there, stunned. *Work. Finally.* "I, I'd be honored, sir," I replied. "When shall I start? And who shall train me?"

His laughter returned, the smile so bright as to make the sun jealous. "There are no others, James," he told me, reaching across to pat my knee, which jerked instantly upon contact. "I have need of little, you see. My food is delivered once a day; you simply must heat it. The cleaning is done once a week while I am asleep. If something needs fixing or mending, I call on the appropriate person from the nearby village."

My eyes again locked with his. *So much blue.* "Then what, Charles, are you hiring me to do exactly?"

He paused as he leaned in, face close enough that I could feel his breath on me. Even that was intoxicating. "Call it a valet, if you will. A trusted houseman." The pause repeated itself, hanging over us as it swirled inside my head. "And I hope I can trust you, James."

I nodded. "Absolutely, sir," I replied. "Absolutely."

His nod mirrored my own. "That we shall soon see, James. That we shall soon see."

The words ran through me like a blade, but still I nodded, smiled, followed him again as he gave me a tour of the castle, from room to astonishing room, each one more finely appointed than the previous one. Mine was the last on the tour. Down the hall from his. It was smaller than the others, but still a far cry from whence I'd come. He pointed to a bell on the wall. "I can ring you from any room in the house, James. All I ask is that you come when called for. Beyond that, your time is your own. Is that to your liking?"

His smile was beguiling, if not downright confusing. Still, it was, as he put it, to my liking. After all, what was not to like? "Yes, Charles. And thank you."

He nodded. "No, James. Thank you." And with that,

he left me there, closing the door behind him. Gone but not forgotten. It was as if he was already etched inside of me. A hole filled that I did not know existed. Yet there were recesses to that hole. Deep, dark places I could feel, pulsing from behind a wall of black. *What*, I thought to myself as I put my belongings away, *shall I be trusted with?*

That I would have to wait to find out.

Though not all that long.

And so I worked. Or so it was called. In fact, it was little like work. If the bell rang, I would seek him out. He was generally in the study or the kitchen. If it was the former, he simply wanted company while he read. If the latter, someone to dine with. Occasionally, we took walks together. He asked of my past, but gave little in regards to his own. He had no guests or visitors aside from the people he employed, and, as for them, I had little contact. In fact, he had become my entire world, and I his.

Two weeks into my employ, we were walking around the gardens, the smell of flowers everywhere, bees buzzing to and fro as birds took wing from the giant oaks all around us. Charles walked close to me, his arm occasionally brushing my own, each time sending a jolt down my spine. Midway through, however, he stopped, turned, and gazed down at me, blue eyes sparkling like sapphires, mesmerizing.

"I'll need you tomorrow, James," he told me, a catch to his voice, a look on his face I hadn't seen before.

"An errand?" I asked. "Some chore?"

He looked away and returned to walking. I kept his pace and waited for his reply. "I trust you, James. Already. Which is a good thing," he said as he stared off into the distance. His pace was steady, though his demeanor seemed suddenly off. "Tomorrow will be a test of that trust." He stopped and turned to look at me, the now-familiar spark rumbling through me. "A test that all before have failed."

I nodded, though I hadn't a clue as to what he was talking about. "I hope to prove that your trust is well-founded then, sir," I replied. "I believe it to be, at any rate."

He smiled and patted my back; the walk continued. "Circumstances have a way of turning things on their sides sometimes," he whispered, rather cryptically, in return.

We walked the rest of the way in silence, though my head was now spinning. *What is this test he speaks of? And what if I fail?*

I didn't have long to ponder on it. The next night arrived, and with it, his promised request.

The bell rang just after dinner while I lay in bed reading one of his many books. I hopped up and put on my night clothes, then went in search of my master. He wasn't, I soon discovered, in any of his usual haunts. Instead, I found him in the rear pantry, a look of lament, of dread, plastered on his otherwise stunning face.

"It is time," he said.

"Time for this test you mentioned?"

He nodded. "Follow me, James," he said.

I followed him to a door off to the side. In the past, I'd discovered that it had always been locked. That night, he opened it and walked through. And down. For the stairs seemed to lead to a basement that I was previously unaware of. He lit the wall candles when we reached the bottom, and once my eyes grew accustomed to the dimness, I saw that the room was small and sparse. The only stick of furniture was a metal cot dead-center, ropes dangling off the sides. I squinted and noticed that the strange item had been bolted to the floor. Then I gulped.

"For me?" I asked, my voice practically lodging in my throat as a pit the size of a lemon formed in my belly.

Except he shook his head. "For me," he replied instead.

"I... I don't understand," I told him, looking from the cot to him and back again.

He walked farther inside and stood by the metal bed. "That is where the trust comes in," he said. "You simply must do as I say and not ask any questions. If you can do that, then all will be fine."

I stood there staring at him as he kicked off his slippers. "And if I cannot?"

He leaned against the cot and rolled off his stockings, his feet now bared. "You must, James," he replied, his fingers working their way down his nightshirt, his chest revealed, a dense matting of hair, two pink nipples jutting out, muscle and sinew etched throughout. His chest rose and fell as he dropped the shirt to the stone floor. He glanced up at me and smiled as he untied his pants before dropping them to the ground as well, then kicked them to the side, until he stood before me, naked, a Greek statue come to life, perfect in every way. "Now tie me to the cot, James."

I froze, my feet planted to the cold stone ground. *Tie him to the cot?* "I, I don't understand, sir," I squeaked out.

"Tie me to the cot, James," he repeated as he hopped up before lying prone atop it, like a corpse on a slab.

It gave me the chills just to look at him. Still, if this was the test he'd mentioned, I had no intention of failing. Not it nor him. And so, reluctantly, I walked over and grabbed the first dangling cord, which I tied to his right foot. "Like this?" I asked.

"Tight," he said, staring down at me and I up at him.

"It must be tight. Tight as you can make it, James."

I pulled on the rope until the knot I'd made was as secure as possible. Charles winced but nodded his head just the same. And so I moved to his other foot, to another rope, tying it as I had the first one. Tight. Tight until the flesh around his ankle turned red as a beet. Tight until his legs were locked in place. This I repeated on both his hands. When finished, I looked at him, my face damp with sweat despite the coldness of the room. "As you wish, sir," I said. "Now what?"

He smiled, his eyes ablaze. "Return in the morning, James. Return and unleash me."

"But you will catch your death of cold down here," I couldn't help but say.

His smile remained. "Fear not, James. Just do as I ask. And do not return until the morning."

I nodded, sensing that the others before me had failed in either the first part of the test or the second. I, suffice it to say, would fail in neither. And so I too smiled and nodded, staring down the length of his hirsute body, at the wiry, black bush in the center, at his soft member, which dangled over his thigh. I sighed and replied, "I will be back in the morning, Charles, and I will untie you then."

He shut his eyes, the grin remaining. I backed out of the room and returned to my bedroom, eager for the night to drain itself out, for me to free him from his bondage. I prayed he'd still be alive when that time occurred.

I slept restlessly. And when the first beams of sunlight wormed their way through my shades, I leapt up from my bed and sped to the pantry and then down to the basement. The candles had gone out, so I lit new ones, then sucked in my breath when I saw him. He was as I'd left him, no worse the wear, though motionless and fully erect, his cock stiff as a board, rising high above his perfect body as if on guard.

Had the sleep of death taken its stranglehold on him? I exhaled as I approached, my hand on his neck. He did not move, did not stir as my hand traveled across his chest, though the dense forest of hair, across the acres of muscled belly, my cock now as rigid as his, my eyes glued to the towering mast. And still my hand went farther south, the hairs of his bush tickling my fingers, fingers that were soon grasping his pole.

And with that, he stirred at last.

"James," he said with a yawn. "Good morning." He stared down at my hand and then to my eyes and then to the tenting in my bed clothes. "What, pray tell, are you doing down there?"

I coughed, my face red. "Seeing if you were still alive, Charles."

He chuckled. "The doctor seems not to check for my pulse down there, James."

Considering he was still smiling and his cock was still rigid in my grip, I too chuckled. "It seemed the most filled with blood, though, sir. Hence my ministrations." Said ministrations had since picked up speed, my fist jacking his prick now, until a translucent bead appeared atop the bulbous head. "Shall I untie you now?"

He moaned, the sound rumbling through his body and out my own. "What for?" he replied. "You seem to have matters well in, um, *hand*."

Said hand moved down his prick and back up his belly, which was now steadily rising and falling, before landing on his chest. I bent down, my face to his. "Sir, am I to understand that you enjoy this?"

His moan grew louder, his eyelids fluttering as I tweaked his nipple in between thumb and index finger, my cock pulsing at the sound of it. He then looked up at me. "It is sometimes, well, pleasant not to be in control, James. If you catch my drift."

Indeed I did. I yanked his nipples this time, his back arching atop the cot. I leaned my face in farther, until my breath and his were as one. "And sometimes pain can be, as you said, *pleasant* as well?" With my free hand, I gave his cock a thwack, then landed my palm on his stomach, the sound pinging around the small room.

His eyes locked on to mine, as they had a habit of doing, until the blue was all-enveloping. "Pleasant, James, seems such a gross understatement at a time like this."

I closed the gap between our faces, taking his lower lip between my teeth. I pulled on the tender, pink flesh and then released it. "Quite." I then mashed my mouth into his, our tongues entwined. Our roles, it seemed, had suddenly been reversed, what with him now at my disposal. And so the kiss grew intense, lingered for what seemed an eternity. But still, there was work to be done.

I pulled my face from his, spit dripping down his chin. I licked it off, my mouth working its way lower, sucking on his neck, until he squirmed beneath me. And still lower I went, my lips around a nipple, teeth grinding into it, his moan the loudest yet, drowned out by my hand coming down hard on his chest, again, and yet again, all while I sucked and slurped and bit away. He fought against the ropes, but, of course, they were tight, as he'd commanded.

My mouth released his nipple, only to wander ever more. I slapped and spanked my way down his body, pulling at the hairs that fairly covered him, all the while seeking out my destination. Hungry for it, I soon sank my lips down and around his leaking head, the salty jizz stinging the back of my throat.

His moan was replaced with a sigh and then a whimper as I yanked on his heavy balls. "You don't play fair, James," he said, huffing now, voice raspy.

I stared up at him, through all that hair and skin and muscle. I twisted as I yanked this time. Once more his eyelids fluttered in response. "There is no joy without pain, Charles," I reminded him, his prick popping out of my mouth.

He sighed and replied, "Then I am due an abundance of joy."

"As am I," I readily agreed, again devouring his cock, taking it down as far as I could before a gagging tear dripped down my cheek. Contentedly I sucked away, all while I pulled on his sac, twisting it this way and that, the ropes keeping him firmly in place.

"Perhaps two can play this game?" he eventually suggested, panting now.

Again I pulled my mouth away from its succulent prize. "The game is so much more fun with two, Charles," I told him, dropping my night pants to the ground, the beast within swaying to and fro, happy at last to be free.

I walked back to the top of the cot and carefully hopped on, glad that it could hold our combined weight. Then I place one foot on the side of his head, the other on the opposite side, until I was straddling him. Meaning the only place to go was down. And so I sank my ass onto his face.

Again he chuckled. "This is a side of you I only ever dreamed of seeing, James."

I squatted farther, rubbing my hole onto his mouth as I slapped my dick against his chin. "And did you also dream of tasting said side, Charles?" I retorted.

Judging by the way his tongue was now working its way inside my hole, the answer to that was a resounding yes. While he ate, I happily jacked away, staring down at his pole of a prick, at his magnificent body, tied up as it was. Still, it was rapture mixed with a tinge of something else, curiosity and sadness, a bit of foreboding. Because why was he down there in the first place? And where had the others before me disappeared to?

In any case, I didn't have long to ponder all this. With his tongue buried deep inside my asshole and my fist pounding furiously away, I was quick to shoot. I threw my head back and a moan escaped from between my lips that swirled around the two of us like a cyclone as my body quaked and my cock spewed. A steady stream of aromatic spunk shot out, splattering his chest and belly, gobs of it pouring over his sides and onto the cot below as I shook every last drop of it out, panting all the while.

Spent, I hopped off the cot and again walked to his side, his eyes on me, boring through. "Am I to stay tied down here at your beck and call now?" he asked, the smirk returning to his face.

I reached for the rope that was tied to his closest foot and set to work on unknotting it. "Nice as that sounds, Charles, I know my place."

He merely nodded and watched, the knot releasing its hold a few minutes later, his one leg freed. I lifted it up and shook it out for him, his balls bouncing, cock swaying. I pushed his knee up to his chest and stared down at his winking hole. Then I ran my fingers around the satiny ring, giving it a spank. He groaned and rasped, "And how about that place down there, James?"

I bent down and spat at the bull's eye, spit tricking down his crack. "Also nice, Charles," I replied, gently sliding a finger inside, his back arching as he sucked in his breath. A second digit joined the fray, both of them working their way in and up and back, his smooth, muscled interior gripping around them until he relaxed and allowed the intrusion.

I grabbed for his prick with my free hand, his leg staying where it was of its own accord. He moaned, long and low and deep, as I slowly drew my fingers in and out, in and out, all while jacking his club of a cock. All this I looked away from, however, opting instead to swim in those pools of blue, which shimmered in the dim candlelight.

He stared back, breathing loudly now, until seconds later he shot, his sweat-drenched body spasming, bucking, rocking, his massive load shooting up and then down, joining mine on his chest and belly. I kept jacking as he writhed beneath me in both pleasure and agony. "Please, James," he pled.

I smiled and released my grip on him. "As you wish, sir," I replied, knowing that our roles would soon be reversed again.

Many minutes later, the ropes again dangling off the cot, Charles standing before me, that's just what they were. He reached out and pulled me in, our lips again joined, his soft as a cloud, as down. I melted into his hairy, sticky body as the time ticked by. Then he pulled away and said, "Thank you."

I nodded. "So I passed this test of yours?"

His nod mirrored my own. "You passed, James." The nod stopped, the smile only briefly faltering. "Though once a month this scene must repeat itself. Once a month you must tie me to the cot and leave me down here until morning."

I shivered, the cold of the room once again finding my bones. "And... and the rest of it?" I couldn't help but ask.

He stroked my cheek, my neck. "That is up to you, James," he replied.

I held his hand and led him up the stairs. "As you wish, sir," I said, yet again, shutting the door behind us.

At least for the time being.

And so began our routine. For the months that ensued, I was the dutiful servant, doing as he asked. But those other times, that one day a month, I would tie him down and have my way with him the next morning. He was mine then, those hours when he was at my disposal, to do with as I pleased. And pleased I did. My cock replaced my fingers or found its way to his mouth. Or his prick worked its way up my ass as I rode him on that cot of his, always tied up, always, until he was once again the lord of the manor, the roles reversed, the pendulum swinging back.

It was never talked of. All of it was simply understood. It was his way, and so it became my own.

Until one fateful day we did indeed have need to discuss it.

A royal page arrived with a flier for Charles, parchment wrapped in a red ribbon. As we never had company apart from the help, which always arrived like clockwork, I sensed that something, either good or bad, was about to occur.

Charles took the parchment from me and grinned as he read what was written upon it. Then he stared up, seemingly calculating something in his head. The grin vanished as quickly as it had arrived.

"What does it say?" I asked, very nearly breathless in anticipation.

"I have been invited by the king to a masquerade ball," he replied, his voice even. Still, he looked frightened. And that was not an emotion I'd ever seen on him before. Needless to say, it didn't suit him.

"Do you not dance, Charles?" I asked, trying to lighten the mood. "No costume? A dislike of crowds? Of music?"

And still he did not smile. Instead, he handed me the invitation. I looked at it, at the date, and my mind began the same calculation that his had just completed. In a flash, my own smile vanished.

"You understand?" he asked.

"It is the night... the basement night," I replied, thinking of a way of putting it without actually saying it.

For some reason, I knew not to talk of it, not in the words that could cause him pain.

"Yes," he said, his eyes on mine, locking on without a blink.

"And you cannot skip that night down there?" I asked.

"No," he said.

"And you cannot miss the ball?" I added.

"No," he echoed. "When the king invites you, you attend."

"Then I shall go in your place, Charles," I told him. "It is a masquerade ball, after all. I will just pretend to be you."

His smile at last returned, radiant in all its beauty, though sad looking just the same. "I thank you for the offer, James, but it would not matter. I am a great deal taller than you. Your pretense would not work. Even your voice is different." Then he pointed to his eyes. "And even behind a mask, your brown could not replace my blue." Thankfully, though the news was dire, his smile remained. "But you could be my date." He put his hand on my shoulder. "Would you like to meet the king, James?"

My heart leapt to my throat. "The king?" I croaked out. "But would it not look odd, your servant as your date? And a male servant at that?"

He shrugged. "It is assumed that I am frail, hence my infrequent appearances." His smile grew northward on his face. "We will just add nurse to your list of duties then."

But still I had to ask, "And that will solve your problem, sir?"

Again he shrugged. "We will have to wait and see, I suppose." Then he sighed. "Wait and see."

Though we didn't have long to wait.

The ball came soon enough. Charles got dressed in all

his fineries. As for me, I simply borrowed from him, the tailor rung for to make the necessary adjustments. Then Charles found us a couple of masks, his all in gold, mine in silver. We were, it seemed, a very handsome couple. Though a nervous couple at that.

The carriage arrived a short while later. It was my first trip outside the castle in all that time. And so I stared out the window, at the trees as they past by, listening to the horse's hooves as they clomped down the dirt road that led to the royal abode many miles away.

Before we arrived, Charles tapped me on the shoulder. "I must make this appearance," he told me.

"I know," said I.

"But there will come a point in the evening when I must leave," he quickly added.

"Will I know this point?" I asked, a gulp riding up and down my throat.

"You will know, James," he replied, his hand on mine, the spark ignited, as it always was with him. "But then you will be in grave danger, I'm afraid." He then reached inside his vest and removed a small pistol that I'd not seen before. "You must use this," he said, handing me the weapon. "You will have no other choice, should the need arrive."

I simply nodded. I had no idea what need he was referring to, nor did I think he would tell me should I ask. In any case, I knew not to ask. He trusted me for a reason. And that trust was well-earned.

And so we entered the castle, to the great ballroom deep within, as dusk fast approached. His name was announced to those in attendance. All eyes turned and stared our way, the participants clearly intrigued at the new guest's arrival. They did not stare for long, though, as that would've been the height of impropriety, but still I knew their eyes were upon us the entire evening.

"You seem to get more attention than the king himself," I whispered into his ear.

"Perhaps they stare at you, James," he replied, his breath hot in my ear. "You are, after all, quite handsome."

I chuckled. "Or at least my mask is."

His mouth remained, the breath ever hotter. "Oh, you are quite handsome, James." My heart skipped a beat, and then skipped again several hours later when the king's retinue found its way to us.

"Charles," the grand, old man said, his hand held out, his mask covered in gems atop a field a regal crimson.

"Sire," said my employer, his own hand held out. "Thank you for the kind invitation." He then turned to me. "And may I present to you my nurseman, James Turner."

All time seemed to stand still as I shook the king's hand, until all I could hear was the beating in my chest, as the music, the chatter, got suddenly drowned out. But then Charles' hand was gripping my arm. So tight I almost yelped. I bade the king thank you for the nice evening and moved away, quickly, with Charles close behind.

"Are you all right?" I asked as we hurried to a set of rear doors.

"No, James," he replied. "And you must get me out of here, now."

We moved quicker, the doors opened for us as we stole into the night, Charles now running through the trees, the forest illuminated by the giant, silver orb high in the sky. I ran behind him, trying as best I could to keep up, panting as sweat streamed down behind my mask.

A mile later, he stopped, turned. "You must return home," he said, his voice forced, deep, gravelly. "Now."

I shook my head. "I cannot leave you out here, Charles."

He sank to his knees. "You must," he groaned. "Before

it is too late."

I got on the ground with him, inches way. And then I removed his mask, recoiling in shock, in horror, because his face was fast becoming something else entirely. And then I stared upward, at the full moon overhead, and at last I understood. "Will I make it in time?" I asked, jumping to my feet.

He stared up, eyes a glowing yellow. "No," he grunted.

I grabbed for the pistol and pointed it his way, but it trembled in my hand. "I... I cannot shoot you, Charles," I said, a tear trickling down my cheek.

He growled, a muzzle where once there was a nose, teeth suddenly bared, rows and rows of them, glinting in the moonlight. "You must. Now," he said, his voice not his own, not like anything I'd ever heard before.

I stood in place, unable to move. "You knew it would come to this," I said. "Either you would kill me, or I you."

Slowly he rose, fighting, I could tell, to retain a semblance of composure. "Yes," he growled, saliva dripping down from his gaping maw.

In that instant, his blue eyes, the last vestiges of his former self, pierced through all that dense hair, locking on to mine, as they always did. And in that moment, when either he would pounce or I would open fire, a third option suddenly presented itself.

"Change me," I whispered, the forest deathly silent save for those two words. Again he growled, shaking his giant mane of hair. Clearly, he heard me, but did he understand what I was asking? "I, I love you, Charles. So either change me or kill me."

He paused, if only for an instant, while the last remaining human part of him was still present, and then, gratefully, chose the former.

For I certainly could not kill him.

It took a single bite and then a hasty retreat on his

part, because, for a werewolf, one bite always leads to so many more. As I would discover, in time. And then my change took hold, as the hairs sprouted and my bones morphed and my face changed from human to wolf. I stared up at the sky, the moon glowing, vibrating, holding on to me as Charles' eyes always seemed to do. At that moment, a stupendous howl roared up from my lungs, shaking the very forest around me. A similar howl arose from some distance away as my brain switched off and my memory collapsed in on itself.

Thankfully, I awoke the next day, my clothes tattered, my body in one piece. I was on the lawn behind our castle, with Charles by my side staring down at me, so much blue as to take my very breath away. He stroked my cheek and smiled. "Are you all right?" he asked.

I pushed myself up on my elbows. "Never better," I replied, really and truly meaning it. In fact, I felt newly reborn. Better. Stronger. And by the throbbing of my cock, even more virile.

He gave it a squeeze as I groaned. "Yes, I can see that." Then he closed the gap, the kiss perfect, long, deep. "Wolves mate for life, you know."

I nodded and wrapped my arms tightly around him. "As you wish, Charles," I told him.

A lone tear streaked down his cheek. "Oh, how I wish for it, James," he replied, the kiss repeated again and again and again. "Oh, how I wish for it."

End.

Alpha Prime
by Katherine Halle

Christian crumpled the thick, cream-colored card in his hand and threw it angrily across the room. He leaned back in his chair, resting his head on the back of it, staring up at the ceiling of his bedroom, the words from the invitation still swimming in front of him.

You are cordially invited to attend
The 20th Annual Cane Masquerade Ball
Hosted by Stephen Cane
Date: August 24
Time: 8 p.m. until ?
RSVP via e-mail: StephenCane.admin@yahoo.com
Attire: Black tie or Costume,
Mask mandatory until midnight

Christian squeezed his eyes shut, trying to blot out the words. Stephen Cane, with his coffee-colored eyes, curly black hair, naturally tanned skin, and perpetual five o'clock shadow, was the biggest, most narcissistic asshole on the planet. He had a reputation for being a lothario and had a string of past lovers littered throughout New Orleans to prove it. Considering that wolves were naturally monogamous, Christian thought his behavior was outrageous. That reason alone was enough to make

Christian want to avoid the ball at all costs, but he knew he'd have to attend, even if only for appearance's sake.

Their community was small, and he had his own reputation to uphold. His parents would insist on his attendance. It didn't matter that he was two years out of college, going to veterinary school, working his way through as a vet tech and old enough to be calling his own shots. Tradition was tradition, and there were certain things he couldn't go against, even if he wanted to. So to the ball he would go and most likely hate every rotten minute of it.

He wallowed for a few more minutes until he heard his computer beep with an incoming message. Christian sat up, not wanting to feel the hope rising in his chest, but unable to help it. A smile broke out over his face, dimpling his cheeks, when he saw the IM request. Quickly he opened it up and had to choke back a laugh when he saw the first comment.

Wolfsbane15: Did u get that stupid invite 2?

He bit his lip and typed a reply.

*DocWolf24: Yup *sigh**

Wolfsbane15: Why the dramaz?

*DocWolf24: *Rolls eyes* rents making me go or I'd skip it like last 6 yrs*

Wolfsbane15: um dude, aren't u like old or smth?

DocWolf24: Fuck u, u going?

Wolfsbane15: yes, same deal, rents

DocWolf24: Hi pot, I'm kettle. STFU >: o

Wolfsbane15: Hey, maybe we cld finally meet

Christian stared at the screen, his heart pounding. They'd been chatting in a shifter chat room for several years now and had become more than just chat buddies. Even though they'd never met in real life and he didn't know Wolfsbane15's real name, he considered the guy a friend. He'd heard all the warnings about people on the internet, but the dude had told him shit that just couldn't be made up. They chatted, they e-mailed, they even texted back and forth, but never once had they talked on the phone, sent a picture of themselves, or even contemplated meeting in real life. Until now.

Wolfsbane15: u still there?

DocWolf24: Yeah, sry, u really want 2 meet?

Wolfsbane15: don't u?

Sitting back, Christian chewed on his thumb, resisting the urge to run a hand through his hair. Did he want to meet Wolfsbane15? There was part of Christian that did, that wanted to find out if the physical package was half as attractive as the online persona. But then the other part screamed out that if the guy wasn't, it could ruin what they had, and what they had was too important to him.

Wolfsbane15: look, we'll hv masks on 'til mid. Wld b like this only in person

Christian's heart slowed down a bit, and he thought about it, picturing it in his head: the two of them dancing, masks on, finally getting to hear his friend's voice. And just like that he made his mind up.

DocWolf24: Let's do it

Wolfsbane15: \m/ I'll let u know abt my costume as soon as I figure it out

DocWolf24: Same

Wolfsbane15: Can't wait

The beeping of his phone startled Christian, and he grabbed it, sighing when he saw it was his mom calling.

DocWolf24: MTE gotta jet tho, rents calling Laterz

Wolfbane15: Laterz

DocWolf24 is offline

"Hey, mom."

"Hi, sweetheart."

"Yes, I got it."

"What?"

"The invitation."

"Oh, good. Have you thought about a costume yet?"

Another sigh escaped, and he hoped his mom hadn't heard it.

"Honey, I know you don't like these things--"

"Then why do I need to go?" he interrupted her.

His mom was silent for a few brief moments. "Christian, honey, you know why you have to go. We've been able to get you out of it for the last few years because of school and all, but--"

"But I'm still in school."

"Yes, but you're local now, have been for almost two years. Last year, you were excused because you had to work and had some sort of clinical, but this year..."

Her voice trailed off, and Christian knew exactly what she was thinking. Stephen's parents had died in the past year, leaving him as Alpha Prime for their region. This was going to be his first time hosting an event this big by himself. It was expected that all the local families who were invited would attend, and Christian's family was no different. As heir to his father's pack, he was not only expected to attend, he was expected to pay homage to Stephen and actually be polite. It made him feel like sticking hot pokers in his eyes.

"Don't worry, Mom, I got it handled. I'm gonna call Cherry for help with my costume. I've already got something in mind, and no, I'm not going to tell you. It will be a surprise."

"Christian," his mom warned.

He rolled his eyes. "Seriously, Mom, don't worry. I'm not going to embarrass myself or you, okay? I do know my responsibilities, and I'm not going to shirk them. I may not like it, might even hate it a little, but I'm gonna do it, okay?"

"I know you would never do that, honey. I really do.

Okay, enough about that. Are you coming to dinner tomorrow night? I'm making your favorite."

Christian's heart lightened and he smiled, leaning back in his chair. "Yeah? What time?"

"Six."

He glanced quickly at his calendar. "I get out of class at five-thirty, so I should be able to make it, no problem."

"Okay, hon, we'll see you then. Love you."

"Love you," and the line went dead.

Christian heaved yet another sigh and set his phone on his desk, leaning back, staring up at the ceiling once more. He'd have to call Cherry and talk to her about his costume idea and see if she could work some magic in the next two weeks. He glanced at his computer to see if Wolfsbane15 was on, but he was definitely offline. Christian shut his computer down and went off to take a shower, and soon after he was in bed, staring at the ceiling again, thinking about Wolfsbane15.

All Christian knew about Wolfsbane15's looks was that he was tall, over six feet, and had brown eyes. All he'd told Wolfbane15 about himself was that he was five eleven, had brown eyes, short, spiky, brown hair and was small but wiry. The only pictures they'd exchanged had been of their desks. He knew Wolfsbane15 was an only child, lived by himself, shifted to a wolf—after all they'd met in a wolf chat room—and had always been attracted to guys.

They'd started out flirting and had settled into a comfortable online companionship, but Christian would have been kidding himself if he didn't sometimes wonder about the possibility of more. However, since Wolfsbane15 had never mentioned it, Christian refused to even think about it. But now, with the suggestion that they meet at the Masked Ball of the year, Christian was having all kinds of thoughts about it, thoughts that made his breath hitch and his dick hard. He palmed his erection through his pajama bottoms, easing some of the tension before rolling onto his side, closing his eyes and trying to chase some sleep.

"Hey, Cherry baby, how are you?"

"Peachy. Whatchu want, darling?"

Christian laughed. "Why do you think I want something?"

Cherry snorted. "Because you only call this early in the morning when you want something. Now, you gonna tell Mama Cherry what it is you need?"

"You know me too well."

"Yeah, so lemme guess, you need me to work some costume magic."

Laughter bubbled up out of Christian again. "How'd you know? Wait, you got an invite, too?"

"But of course. You think good ol' Stephen would leave out the prettiest drag queen in town?"

"Well, when you put it that way, how could he?"

"Damn straight... well, not exactly straight." Cherry laughed.

"Fuck you."

"Such language. So you got a date for this shindig?"

Christian could feel his cheeks heating up, and he hesitated before answering.

"Oh, OH. You do! Are you holding out on Mama Cherry?"

"No. NO!" Christian protested. "It's just, remember that guy I've been chatting with? Wolfsbane?"

"The one in the shifter chat room you were telling me about? The one who sounds tall, dark, handsome, and mysterious?"

"Yeah, that one. He wants to meet at the ball. Said we'll have masks on, so it will kind of be like we're on the computer. At least until the reveal at midnight. He said if we decide not to pursue something further, we can part ways before midnight and never reveal ourselves. Just go back to being chat buddies."

Cherry was silent for a moment, almost to the point of making Christian nervous, before she finally spoke up again. "Well, okay then, we're just gonna have to get you all prettied up so you can snag that man. Did you have something in mind?"

"I do. Can I come over later and discuss it?"

"You're gonna keep me in suspense?"

"Let's just say I want to keep it as private as possible because it's going to make a statement."

"Sounds delicious! Okay, you can keep your secrets for now. When do you wanna meet?"

"You free later today? I have to work until noon and then have a class at two. Maybe I can come over and we can grab some lunch?"

"It's a date, sugar."

"Thanks, Cherry."

"Anytime, darling. Now get your cute ass to work!"

"Yes, ma'am. Bye."

"Ciao!"

Christian thumbed his phone off, grabbed his bag and headed out the door.

Wolfsbane15 has logged on
Wolfsbane15: Doc? You there?
DocWolf24: Yup, what's up?
Wolfsbane15: school go ok?
DocWolf24: yeah, work for you?

Wolfsbane15: Yeah. So…

DocWolf24: got my costume figured out, friend is working on it

Wolfsbane15: Yeah? What is it?

DocWolf24: it's a surprise

Wolfsbane15: how will I know who u r?

Christian laughed.

DocWolf24: I'll tell u that nite what abt u?

Wolfsbane15: 2 can play that game

DocWolf24: Fucker

Wolfsbane15: LOL All's fair and all

Heart stuttering in his chest, Christian chewed on his bottom lip. He wondered if he should go where this could be leading and decided to go for broke. He was taking a bit of a risk with his costume. Might as well risk his heart, too.

DocWolf24: Is this love or war?

Wolfsbane15: What do u want it 2 b?

Christian's fingers paused over the keyboard. He clenched his right hand into a fist and licked his lips nervously, his heart pounding. What did he want it to be?

DocWolf24: Not war

Wolfsbane15: Was hoping u'd say that

Relief flooded Christian's body, and his lips curled up into a smile. He stretched back into his chair, flexing his hands before typing a response.

DocWolf24: yeah?

Wolfsbane15: yeah

DocWolf24: for realz?

Wolfsbane15: LOL yeah for realz, what r u 12?

DocWolf24: shut up fucker LOL

Wolfsbane15: So, we doin this?

DocWolf24: Yeah, yeah, I think we r, ok?

Wolfsbane15: More than

DocWolf24: Good, good

Wolfsbane15: So plans for the rest of the nite?
DocWolf24: Hv 2 study u?
Wolfsbane15: nml stuff
DocWolf24: boring
Wolfsbane15: LOL trufax
DocWolf24: better go
Wolfsbane15: laterz
DocWolf24: bye
Wolfsbane15 has logged off

Stephen scowled at his reflection in the mirror. He hated this costume, and not just the full lion mane fitted and attached to the mask of a regal lion's face. The color of the brown suit it topped was just as awful; it was washed out and completely out of date. It was the traditional costume for the Alpha Prime, so he was expected to wear it. It fit him perfectly, of course, having been altered shortly after his father's death, just like everything else. But as he looked at himself in the mirror, he didn't feel like the Alpha Prime. He felt like a sheep in wolf's clothing.

His fists clenched, he turned, looking himself up and down. Stephen knew what was expected of him, but he'd made some cautious inquiries and talked to a few of the Council members he knew he could trust to back him up. He was planning on making a few changes, the first being this ridiculous costume. He took the headdress off and threw it into the chair in disgust.

He ran a hand through his thick, black hair and growled in frustration. Only ten more days until the ball and he didn't have a costume. He wanted something understated, classy, regal, not showy, trendy, or tacky. Cherry was the best in the business, but she hated him, or rather treated him with barely disguised contempt. Not that Stephen could blame her.

He did have a bit of a reputation; one that he'd intentionally fostered. It was all fake, of course, but only a select few knew that. The Alpha Prime had to appear, well, Alpha, and a few Council members believed the best way to do that was to leave a string of past lovers. No one had any complaints or anything bad to say about him, other than the fact that he was a player. A few members of the Council appreciated that, thought it showed his strength, thought it would show a future mate that he was virile. Those select few also seemed to think that his father's death meant a change of ideals and had tried to use him to push their own agenda. Up to this point, he'd gone along with them, but no more. He was done trying to fit into their mold. Just a few more people behind him and he'd have all the support he needed to do things his way.

Which was why, since his father's death, he'd been slowly and quietly working to gain support from others on the Council, others who felt as he did, as his father had. Then, after he chose a mate and took his rightful spot as head of the Council, he would change a few things, starting with kicking out every last one of the old guard and bringing in fresh blood with a new vision, a better vision.

First, he had to get through this damn Masquerade Ball and somehow find his mate; the Alpha Prime had to have a mate, and Stephen was no different. He could feel the need burning under his skin, felt it more each time there was a new moon. If he didn't find his mate soon, the need would become so great that it would affect his ability to lead. It was imperative he find his quickly. With the new instructions he'd laid out in regards to the ball, he hoped to be able to blend in with the guests and socialize like a normal person, instead of overseeing things like some monarch from a lonely perch up on the dais. That would come later. After the removal of masks and the reveal.

He quickly shed the rest of the old costume, abandoning it in a heap, and changed into a button down shirt and his favorite pair of jeans. His secretary would complain, but he knew she secretly approved of the more casual look. Stephen grabbed his phone off his bedside table, checked his messages, sent a quick e-mail to his secretary confirming and changing bits of his schedule and then, taking a deep breath, he pulled up Cherry's number and dialed.

"To what do I owe this pleasure, Alpha?"

Stephen bit back an angry retort and sighed. "Good morning to you, too, Cherry. I'm going to get right to the point. I need a costume for the ball, and I need you to keep it to yourself."

He heard the sharp indrawn breath on the other end.

"You're not wearing the traditional Alpha Prime costume?"

"No. So, can I come see you? Will you work some magic for me, please?"

Cherry was silent for a moment. "Okay, on one condition; you let me design the costume for you. Trust my judgment."

"But--"

"No buts, I'm very busy, as you can imagine. I'm making a ton of costumes for this ball. Adding one more, especially one that's going to have to be as special as yours, is gonna make me lose sleep trying to get them all done. So, you want me to do it, you go with my vision, which means, we're gonna have to have lunch together and soon."

"Why?"

"Because I can't express my vision of you if I don't know you. All I know is your reputation, and I'm getting the impression that there's more to you than what you've been putting out there. So, this afternoon, okay?"

"Yes, I'll make sure my secretary clears my schedule. Where, what time, and how long do you need?"

"There's a cute little café right next to my shop. We can grab a quick bite there. Then you can come up, and I can get you measured and talk to you about what I see. So, say noon?"

"That's fine."

"See you then, Alpha."

"Cherry?"

"Yes?"

"Thank you."

"Y-you're welcome."

The line went dead, and Stephen thumbed the lock on his phone and slid it into his pocket. His secretary was going to have a fit rearranging his schedule, but it just had to be done. If he was going to make a statement at the ball, he had to do it the right way, and Cherry was it.

He finished getting ready, and snatching the discarded costume off the floor, he raced down the stairs. Stephen stuffed it into the kitchen trash can right on top of the old coffee grounds from the day before. He'd prefer to burn it, but he just didn't have the time. Grabbing some toast and coffee, he ran out the door. His head was filled with his schedule and thoughts on all the meetings he had this morning, including one about his new instructions for the ball. That meeting was definitely going to be interesting.

"What?"

"You want to what?"

"You can't do that!"

"SILENCE!"

Everyone started at Stephen's shouted order, but silence reigned as they gave him their undivided attention.

"Who is the Alpha Prime?" he growled, giving them just a little bit of the Alpha timbre.

When nobody spoke, he continued. "My father always embraced change. He taught me that change was inevitable. The best thing to do was to expect it, to embrace it, and sometimes to initiate it yourself when the time is right. Well, I deem that the time is right. There will be no formal announcing of guests upon their arrival, there will be no dais for me to sit upon, looking down on everyone else enjoying themselves, and we will let guests leave before the reveal at midnight if they so desire."

Stephen held up his hands when one of the older council members opened his mouth to speak.

"I'm not finished yet. I want the ball to be fun, not something people feel they have to endure. Losing some of these old, tired rules frees people up to relax and enjoy the freedom that wearing a mask can bring. It will also allow me to mingle and talk freely with people without them knowing who I am. I'll be able to get a better feel for how things are going in the pack as a whole and what people are thinking."

Understanding started to bloom on the Council members' faces. Smiles began to appear, and Stephen finally felt the tension inside him start to ease. Sure, there were going to be a few holdouts, but it was obvious that he was winning the majority over to his way of thinking. He grinned as excited chatter started up around the table, people throwing out ideas for other things that could be changed for the better. He sat down and leaned back, watching and listening, pleased that so many more than he expected were on board with his plan. It would make getting rid of the few who weren't so much easier.

The meeting concluded quickly after that. Several

members clapped him on the back enthusiastically and offered their support until the last one took his leave and Stephen was finally alone. He glanced at his watch and realized that if he didn't leave soon he was going to be late for his lunch with Cherry and then he would never get his costume. He logged off his computer, said goodbye to his secretary, and took off.

"You're not what I expected at all. I mean, on a one on one basis that is."

Stephen chuckled. "Um, thank you, I think?"

Cherry winked at him, her long, curly, red hair blowing in the breeze. "Oh, honey, that's a good thing. Now tell Cherry why you put out this lothario façade when really that's not what you are at all."

Clenching his glass tightly, Stephen cleared his throat. "I'm not sure I understand what you mean." He smiled tightly.

Cherry rolled her icy blue eyes. "Please, anyone who gets close enough can tell you're not the love 'em and leave 'em type. Maybe that's why you keep everyone at arm's length? Why the big push for this costume, this year, to be different?"

"Because it's my first year being completely in charge. If I want everyone to respect me as Alpha Prime, I have to make it mine, the ball, the role, everything. I can't live in my father's shadow, no matter how much the pack loved him or how good a leader he was. I need to prove myself, show everyone that although I'm his son, I'm my own man and a deserving leader in my own right."

"Okay, I get that, but there's something else." Cherry paused, narrowing her eyes and then surprise registered on her face. "Holy fuck!" she whispered, looking around furtively.

Stephen's heart skipped a beat in his chest, and he shook his head. "No, no. Just NO."

Cherry looked at him sympathetically and reached across the table to squeeze his hand. "Honey, denying it isn't going to change it. You're going into heat. You're gonna have to find your mate soon or--"

"Look, you don't have to tell me the 'or' part. I know. I KNOW. Fuck!" He glanced around quickly, lowering his voice. "Do you think everyone knows? Can everyone tell?"

"Well, you do put off a certain scent, but not everyone knows or recognizes exactly what it means. To the members of the Council, it just means you're Alpha Prime because it's all wrapped up in the scent of you as their leader. To your friends, same thing, it's all wrapped up in your scent as their friend. But to your family, to those of us that are attuned to that scent, and to your future mate? It's like waving a bright red flag. Since your family is gone, I'm guessing you have nobody else close to you who would recognize it."

"So why did you?"

Cherry shrugged her slim shoulders. "Don't know for sure to be honest. I can scent anyone in heat. Always have been able to. It's a part of me. I think it's part of what makes it easy for me to see what a person is underneath their masks. To be able to see their true self."

"That's what makes you so good at what you do," Stephen said softly.

Cherry shrugged and gave him a tiny, embarrassed smile, and Stephen laughed.

"So, what can you do for me?"

"Why don't we finish up here? Let me get you upstairs and start taking measurements, and then we can talk."

Looking around the café and seeing several interested people watching them, he nodded. "Got it."

He signaled the waiter, paid for their lunch, and followed Cherry's tiny, curvaceous form back to her studio. He obediently got up on the block and stood there while Cherry walked around him, looking him up and down and making clucking noises with her tongue.

Stephen looked around the room as she did, his eyes landing on a mannequin draped with a gauzy, white fabric. It was covering a pair of black pants, shot through with silver thread and a white dinner jacket with what appeared to be the same silver thread running through it. Stephen thought he could see the outline of something attached to the back, something with feathers, but he couldn't quite make out what. The outfit was clearly unfinished, but it was going to be breathtaking on whoever wore it. "What's that?"

Cherry glanced over to where he was looking and turned back to him with a cocky grin. "That's a costume I'm working on for a friend."

"What is it? It's gorgeous."

"I'm sure you'll see it the night of the ball. He'll be there."

Stephen's heart tripped over itself in his chest. He could just imagine the man who would be wearing that costume. "He-he'll be there?"

"Yup." Cherry looked up at him, and Stephen swallowed hard, trying to ignore the burning under his skin that had just started up again. Something about the costume called to him, and he couldn't place his finger on it. It was too nebulous and just out of his reach.

"Can I see it when it's finished?"

Cherry stopped measuring him. "Um, I need to talk to my friend. He and I worked hard on the concept, and I think he's hoping to keep it under wraps until he shows up."

Stephen went silent, and Cherry went back to

measuring him. When she finished, she turned to look at him, scrutinizing him and up and down, walking around him and muttering to herself.

"I think you should go as you are."

"What?"

"The Alpha Prime has always gone as a lion in the past, right? King of the beasts? But you're not a lion, you're a wolf. A big, black, gorgeous one if I'm not mistaken."

"How'd you-- never mind."

"So, you should go as you are. I'm thinking an elegant, black tailored suit, and a mask, oh a mask--" Cherry ran off to grab a sketch pad and started drawing.

Stephen watched in silence as she drew. He stood there motionless for almost fifteen minutes before she finally stopped and turned it around to show him. His breath caught in his throat, and his heart started to pound. He could see himself wearing the mask and the black suit and dancing with the mysterious owner of the silvery costume. Stephen licked his lips nervously, his mouth dry.

"Well?"

"It's perfect," Stephen said reverently, holding the sketch in his hands. A gleeful smile broke out over his face as he met Cherry's eyes. "It's exactly what I was hoping for. Thank you!"

Cherry beamed back at him and gently took the sketch out of his hand. "You're welcome. I'll have it ready for the first fitting in a week. That gives us four days to fix it if it needs to be fixed, but it won't. Now, get out of here, I've got work to do."

Laughter bubbled out of Stephen's chest, and he leaned over to kiss Cherry on the cheek, her jasmine scented perfume washing over him. "Thank you, for giving me a chance. And for being discreet."

Cherry waved her hand dismissively. "No worries, Alpha. But I'll tell you this: you need to lose the reputation if you want to find a mate. Whoever he is, you need to be truthful with him, otherwise..."

"Thank you," Stephen said again. "I'll see you in a week."

"Ciao," Cherry responded, already distracted by her work.

Stephen shook his head, smiling, and walked out the door.

Wolfsbane15: Doc, you there?
DocWolf24: Yup
Wolfsbane15: Got my costume sorted 2day
DocWolf24: yeah? What?
Wolfsbane15: not telling, surprise
DocWolf24: But then how will I recognize u?
Wolfsbane15: LOL don't worry I'll find u, ur gonna tell me yours right?
DocWolf24: maybe ;p
Wolfsbane15: tease, not long now
DocWolf24: nope ten days
Wolfsbane15: can't wait
DocWolf24: mte
Wolfbane15: better go, duty calls, chat later 2nite?
DocWolf24: yeah 10ish
Wolfsbane15: Until then
Wolfsbane15 has logged off

Stephen pushed away from his laptop with a smile on his face. These IM conversations were often the highlight of his day, and today was no exception. Although, this time, they were competing with his conversation with Cherry and his immediate response to the white costume. He had an idea why he'd responded the way he did, and he had a feeling Cherry might as well, but she wasn't confirming. He'd be interested in finding out if he had the same reaction next week, provided the costume was still in Cherry's studio. Stephen would have sat there and thought about it all day if not for the interruption of his phone and pack business, which kept him busy the entire rest of the day.

Christian stared at himself in the mirror. The costume was exquisite and just what he'd wanted. A white, gauzy material adorned with silver buttons made up the shirt. Over it he wore a perfectly tailored, white dinner jacket shimmering with silver thread. Black pants shot through with the same silver thread accentuated the long lines of his legs. The mask was an elaborate one covering half his face, sparkling with iridescent sequins and festooned with feathers around the edges. But the most magnificent part was the pair of white feathered wings attached to his back, completing his transformation into a swan. "It's perfect," he whispered reverently.

"I knew you'd love it. Okay, you go ahead and admire yourself for as long as you want; I'm just gonna do a bit of work over here on the side. I'm swamped." Cherry beamed at him.

Turning around, Christian looked over the costume in the three-paneled mirror until something made him pause. Suddenly he was too hot, the costume was constricting, and it was making his skin itch. No, his skin was burning up, or rather *under* his skin was burning up. His heart was pounding, and his dick was growing unreasonably hard in his pants. He could smell something, but he just couldn't place it. Whatever it was, he knew it was the cause of his discomfort. Because it was intoxicating and he couldn't get enough of it, didn't want to get enough of it. He wrinkled his nose up. "What's that smell?"

Cherry spun around, black cloth clutched tightly in her hand, her eyes wide. "What smell?"

Christian clenched his hands into fists. "That smell. Can't you smell it? I need it. Fuck, where is it?"

"Oh shit." Cherry dropped what she was doing and came over to him. "Okay, honey, let's get you out of that costume and into the fresh air."

Within minutes, the costume was back on the dummy, and Christian was changed and outside. Once the fresh air hit him, his body started to relax. The frantic need inside him diminished, and he began to feel normal again. When he did, he stood up and glared at Cherry. "What the hell was that?"

Visibly upset, Cherry wrung her hands. "Damn, sweetie. I had a client the other day. He was going into heat. I had the papers with his measurements out, must have had his scent on them."

"Fuck." Christian's eyes widened. "Fuck, I'm so fucking fucked! Who was it?"

"Honey, I can't tell you." She held up her hands in supplication. "Not because I don't want to. I literally can't tell you."

"Shit," Christian muttered, sitting down in one of the café chairs and putting his head in his hands. "He'll be at the ball then?"

"Most definitely."

"Fuck, I hope we can at least get to a private place."

Cherry came over to him and hugged him. "If it means anything, I think he had a similar reaction. He was just able to control it a bit more." She rubbed her hand up and down his back comfortingly. "Look at it this way, at least you'll have found your mate, and he's an Alpha."

"Yeah, someone I don't know. What if I hate him?"

Cherry pulled back and looked at him intently. "I can

honestly say that once you get to know him, you won't hate him. But you have to give him a chance. Trust Mama Cherry and keep an open mind, okay? Remember that."

Nodding soberly, Christian hugged Cherry. "I better go. I've got some thinking to do, need to talk to my parents, and apparently I better start preparing for the ball and my upcoming mating. Bye, Cherry."

The night of the ball came much too quickly for Christian. He'd barely had time to talk to Wolfsbane15 since the incident at Cherry's. He'd texted the guy earlier that afternoon to tell Wolfbane15 what his costume would be. The only thing he'd gotten in return was a quick text saying Wolfsbane15 would find him at the ball, nothing about Wolfsbane15's costume. It was moot now anyway. As soon as his mate arrived at the ball, he and Christian would be immediately drawn to each other, and once they touched, all bets were off.

As he dressed, he felt a twinge of sadness because he really enjoyed talking with Wolfsbane15. He hoped they could at least continue their friendship; anything else would be out of the question. Once he was mated... well, everyone knew wolves mated for life, or at least were serial monogamists. It would be different for him, though. He couldn't imagine finding a second mate. This would be it for him; he just hoped his mate felt the same way.

Christian stepped back from the mirror and looked himself over one last time before nodding in satisfaction and heading out to the car. The drive to the Cane mansion was too fast and too long, all at the same time. He rubbed his hands nervously on the seat, trying to dry off the sweat he could feel on them. He didn't want to sully his costume. Adjusting the mask on his face, he took a deep breath as the car came to a stop.

Opening the car door, he stepped out, blinking against the flashes. Stephen Cane and his stupid press. There were always photogs at these things, and it was annoying as hell. Christian smiled at them and slogged his way through. He was grateful there would be no formal announcement of his arrival; he'd always hated those. This year the guests were allowed to mingle and meander around the estate, making their way to the ballroom whenever they chose or avoiding it all together.

Christian wished he could do that, but he knew what was required of him and headed straight to the ballroom. He might be wearing a mask, but enough people would recognize his voice that his presence or absence would be noted. Christian thought it best to get his appearance out of the way so he'd be able to enjoy the rest of the night. The closer he got to the ballroom, though, the more his senses started to tingle. The itching and burning under his skin started up again, and he knew his mate had to be there somewhere.

He moved through the crowd gracefully, greeting people, dancing with a few others, all while trying to ignore his body and stay in tune with it at the same time. He spotted Cherry and made his way over to her and was just about to ask her to dance when he felt the hairs on the back of his neck rise. His heart started to pound, and the burning under his skin intensified until it was almost unbearable. Smiling at Cherry, he whispered. "It's him."

She grinned, kissed him on the cheek and wished him the best. "I know. Go get your man, and remember what I said about giving him a chance. Later, sweetheart."

Christian turned and watched as a man in a fitted, black suit with a black wolf mask wove his way through the crowd. He barely stopped to talk to anyone, as if he was on a mission. Christian knew instantly it was his mate. He wondered idly if his mate felt the same desperate need he felt. Hands fisted at his sides, Christian fought the urge to run to the man and wrap himself around him. Granted, that behavior would be accepted in their society—in fact it happened quite frequently when mates finally found each other—but Christian preferred to keep his private life private, and he really hoped his mate did, too.

Then, suddenly, his mate was there, right in front of him. Christian looked up into the warmest brown eyes he'd ever seen. He licked his lips nervously and gave the wolf a tentative smile. He was just about to extend his hand to introduce himself when the man spoke first.

"Doc?"

Shock and relief flooded through Christian. "Wolfsbane? Is that you?"

Strong arms wrapped around him, pulling him into his mate, surrounding him with that intoxicating scent and the burning under his skin eased off a bit.

"Yeah, it's me."

Christian buried his face in Wolfsbane's chest, wrapping his arms around Wolfsbane and fisting his hands into the back of Wolfsbane's jacket. "Oh my gods, you have no idea how happy I am right now. I've been so afraid ever since that day at Cherry's and sad because of you, and now here you are and--"

"Shh, I've got you," Wolfsbane said softly, kissing the side of Christian's head.

Instantly the tension slid right out of Christian's body, and he went pliant in Wolfsbane's arms. "Can we go someplace a bit more private? Please?"

"Yeah, yeah, let's do that, because if you're feeling half of what I'm feeling, I'm thinking our physical restraint won't last much longer."

Christian laughed, although he knew in his heart that

Wolfsbane was right. The burning had eased, but it had shifted into something darker, more primal, the need to mark and to be marked by his mate. The need to make sure his mate smelled only like him and the need to let everyone around them know they were a mated pair.

They made their way through the crowd, holding hands tightly. Christian snuck glances at Wolfsbane, taking in his broad shoulders, his dark hair, the regal way he carried himself. Something about him started to work at Christian's mind. Something that was familiar about him, but Christian couldn't place it. Whatever it was, it didn't matter. Nature had determined they were mates, their blood and their ancestry bringing them together, and soon their own physical needs and desires would link them forever.

Wolfsbane led them out of the ballroom and into the foyer of Stephen's home, where he stopped. They glanced around quickly, and then Wolfsbane started for the stairs, Christian's hand still grasped tightly in his.

"Wait," Christian said breathlessly. "What are you doing? If we get caught--"

"Don't worry, we'll be fine."

"What about Cane?"

Wolfsbane squeezed his hand. "You let me worry about Cane. Right now, I can't wait to get my hands on you."

Christian's dick thought that was an excellent idea as well, so he shut up and let Wolfsbane lead him through the upstairs and back to one of the bedrooms. He looked around while Wolfsbane closed the door behind them. The room was tastefully decorated in blues and greens and a little bit of silver. A huge, king-sized bed was the focal point with a small sitting area off to one side, mirrored by a dressing table on the other.

He glanced around the rest of the room, took in the

walk-in closet standing wide open, the bathroom open but dark, and off in the corner, a desk. His heart started to pound as he walked closer to the desk. The arrangement of pictures on the wall behind the chair looked eerily familiar. He moved over to the desk and stood in front of it, trailing his fingers over the laptop. He looked up at the wall, the chair and then turned to Wolfsbane, staring into those coffee colored eyes and noting again the regal way Wolfsbane stood, and everything finally fell into place.

"I've seen this before, in a picture. This is your desk, but it's in his house. Your eyes, they're his eyes. You're Cane," Christian whispered, his heart hammering in his chest, his blood roaring in his ears. He closed his eyes tightly, hands fisted at his sides. It couldn't be true. Wolfsbane—*his mate!*—couldn't be Stephen Cane, the Alpha Prime, one of the few pack members Christian intensely and very actively disliked.

Feeling a warm hand wrap around his, he swallowed hard. Fingers under his chin tilted his head up. Christian opened his eyes and stared into the brown eyes that just minutes before had felt like home.

"Please don't shut me out," Stephen whispered softly. "I'm still Wolfsbane, still the same guy you chat with. I meant everything I ever said in our conversations. It was the one place I allowed myself to truly be me. No role, no mask, no nothing. Just me."

"But you..." Christian's voice trailed off as he tried to process. "You're... All those men... How--"

A bitter laugh slipped out from behind Stephen's mask. "Don't believe everything you hear." He let go of Christian's hand and turned away, lifting a hand as if to run it through his hair but then dropping it when his fingers touched the mask. "The Alpha Prime has a certain reputation that must be upheld," he intoned by rote.

A mirthless laugh escaped before he continued. "Or so

certain members of the Council have been telling me since my father died. I went along with them because I had a plan, a plan I now have the backing to execute. But then you happened. Who knew I would find my mate just as I was about to change our world?"

He turned back to Christian. "And with you wearing that costume, too. How ironic."

Christian tilted his head in curiosity. "Ironic?"

"They wanted me to prove that the Alpha Prime was virile, hence the rumors and stories of me leaving behind a string of lovers. It's like they forgot that serial monogamy is the true nature of wolves. Something I want to remind them of. And then you, *my mate,* show up dressed as a swan. One of the few animals that actually practices true monogamy. Swans mate for life. It's what I've always wanted. It's what my father had."

Christian moved closer to him. "I don't understand. Your father was a great Alpha Prime. Why would they want to change?"

Stephen shook his head. "It's long and complicated and political, but the short version is that someone on the Council was posturing to take over, someone with a lot of power and very different ideas about how to run things. I had to go along with his desires until I was sure I had enough votes to back me instead of him."

His eyes took on an excited almost desperate edge. "But now, with you by my side, we can make sure that never happens. Your family is powerful, well known and liked within the pack. With you as my mate, we'll have the backing of the people, and that idiot on the Council will have to back down with his tail between his legs."

Christian bit his lip, chewed on it nervously. His mind was swirling, trying to make sense of the information overload. Even worse, underneath it all, his nerves were humming with arousal and the wolf inside him was howling to mate, to mark, *to claim*. He looked up as Stephen started to talk again.

"Look, I know you don't like me, but you do like Wolfsbane, and I can feel your wolf scrambling inside you to get to me. Can you give us a chance? Because I'm afraid if I don't start kissing you now..."

Cherry's words about giving his mate a chance echoed through Christian's head. He took a tentative step forward and reached up, gently pulling the mask off Stephen's face, staring at Stephen intently. Christian dropped the mask on the floor and lifted a hand up, cupping Stephen's cheek. Stephen closed his eyes and pushed into the touch, a sigh escaping his lips and ghosting over Christian's skin.

"You know, a friend told me that when I got to know you, I wouldn't hate you. She made me promise I'd give you a chance. So I'm going to trust her and my wolf, because if you don't kiss me right now, I'm afraid--" The rest of Christian's sentence was cut off when Stephen pulled his mask off, tossed it aside, wrapped his arms around Christian and crushed their mouths together.

Christian opened up as soon as he felt Stephen's tongue probing at his lips. He clutched at the back of Stephen's jacket, pressing into the kiss, thrusting his tongue into Stephen's mouth and tasting him for the first time. Christian could taste hints of fruit, the smoky flavor of whiskey, but mostly what he tasted was *mine*.

Christian's hands slid up Stephen's back, hooking over his shoulders, holding him close. Stephen's hands were in his hair, tugging it, tilting his head just so, ensuring their mouths slotted together perfectly. Stephen's scent was intoxicating, overwhelming Christian's senses. He could feel the wolf inside him, prancing around happily, all set to roll over and bare its belly as soon as Stephen was ready.

Drawing away from the kiss and tugging on his hair

again, Stephen pulled Christian's head back so their eyes met. "Tell me you want this," he rasped out. "Tell me we're doing this, because if we continue I won't be able to stop, not until we're joined and I'm spilling inside you."

Unable to stop a whine from slipping out, Christian tried to pull Stephen closer. "I want this. I *need* this. Fuck, I feel like I'm going to explode if I don't get you inside me right now. I just, fuck, you're my mate, as fucked up as this may be. I can't deny that. I'm not saying everything is perfect, because it's not. I can't agree with anything you said, not now when I can't think clearly. Not when I'm fighting my baser instincts, which are telling me to drop to my knees and pull you down with me, to kiss you until you're buried inside me. So please, can we get back to the kissing and the mating and talk afterward when my brain isn't so foggy?"

He pushed closer to Stephen, rubbing their groins together, feeling the hard length of Stephen's cock through the soft wool of his tailored pants. Stephen growled, wrapped his hand around the nape of Christian's neck and brought their mouths together again, claiming his lips in a searing kiss. He thrust his tongue into Christian's mouth, and Christian shoved a thigh between his legs, rubbing up against Stephen's erection.

"Bed, now," Stephen groaned, breaking the kiss. His hands fumbled at his jacket, jerking it down off his arms.

Christian watched him strip for a split second before reaching for his own costume. Bare-chested, Stephen stretched a hand out to help him, but Christian batted Stephen's hand away. "No, if I ruin this, Cherry will have my ass."

Stephen's eyes darkened as he moved to undo the zip on his pants. "The only one having your ass will be me."

Arousal sparked through Christian, his wolf obviously pleased with Stephen's possessive streak. He willed his fingers to move faster as he stripped out of the white, gauzy material that made up his shirt until he was standing naked before Stephen. His eyes raked over Stephen's muscular form: the taut abs, the dark nipples, and the thick, heavy cock nestled in black hair. Staring for a moment at the base of Stephen's cock, where it was thicker, Christian swallowed hard at the realization that, as Alpha Prime, Stephen would have a knot that would link them together for a short while when they mated.

As if he'd read Christian's mind, Stephen stepped forward and kissed Christian softly. "I promise it won't hurt when it finally goes in. Come on."

Stephen linked their fingers together and pressed him backward toward the bed. When the back of Christian's knees hit the edge of it, Stephen dipped his head and kissed Christian's shoulder. "Get on the bed."

Rushing to comply, Christian spread himself out like an offering in the middle of the bed. His cock was rock hard against his belly, pre-come appearing drop by drop at the head. Eyes locked on Stephen, Christian hoped the naked desire he felt showed on his face. Christian wasn't usually submissive in bed, quite the opposite, in fact, but his wolf was overriding his normal sensibilities and bowing to the Alpha Prime. It was exciting in a way sex had never been before. He wanted Stephen to own his body, to claim him, to *mark* him and let him do the same in return.

Stephen trailed a hand down Christian's chest, circling his nipple before flicking it lightly with his finger. Christian arched up into the touch, and then Stephen was sinking down on top of him, pushing him into the bed, licking up the side of his neck. Turning his head to the side, Christian bared his neck to Stephen. "Do it," he implored. "Mark me."

"This is only the beginning," Stephen said darkly

before sucking Christian's skin in between his teeth.

Fingers digging into Stephen's shoulders, Christian bit his lip as pain blossomed out from where Stephen was biting him. It wasn't hard enough to break the skin, not yet, that would come later, but the pain was white hot in its own way. Just when Christian was getting ready to beg him to stop, Stephen pulled away and licked at the spot, pressing lightly on it with his tongue and sending pain-spiked pleasure shooting through Christian's body, straight to Christian's cock. "Fuck," Christian moaned.

Stephen pulled back and moved down his chest, leaving mark after purple mark until Christian knew his entire torso had to be littered with them. His wolf was so pleased, it was practically convulsing with joy inside him. Stephen must have sensed it because he pulled off the mark he was currently leaving on Christian's hip and let out a deep, throaty chuckle. A frown furrowing his brow, Christian silently scolded his wolf and felt a blush creep up his body.

A stinging slap on his thigh forced his attention back to Stephen. "Hey," Christian cried out indignantly, reaching down to rub at the aching spot.

Stephen's hand shot out and grabbed his wrist before he could reach it. "Don't be angry at your wolf. Let your wolf enjoy this just as much as you are."

Christian struggled against the hold on his wrist, and when Stephen's fingers tightened, it sent a thrill through his body. In less than a second, Stephen was on top of him again, holding both hands above his head, pinning them to the bed. "You like that," Stephen said incredulously.

Another flush stole over Christian's body as he flexed his wrists in Stephen's grip. When Stephen just held him tighter, he finally gave up, huffing out a frustrated sigh. "Okay, yeah, maybe. Just... can we explore my submissive side later? Because it seems to only exist for you; that's never happened before."

"Huh," Stephen mused thoughtfully, rubbing his thumb over the pulse in Christian's wrist. Stephen grinned down at him playfully. "Good to know."

He dipped his head and kissed the side of Christian's mouth, just barely a taste, and when he pulled off, Christian stretched up chasing after Stephen.

"Oh, this is going to be fun," Stephen laughed. "So much fun."

Struggling against Stephen's grip, Christian wrenched his wrists up, trying to shake the hold on them, but Stephen held on even more tightly. Christian bucked his hips, and their cocks rubbed together, causing Stephen to let out a grunt and crush their mouths together.

The wolf in Christian howled with happiness, and Christian moaned into the kiss, giving his wolf voice. He tangled Stephen's tongue with his own, loving the feel of it in his mouth. The hold on his wrists shifted as Stephen let go with one hand. From the way Stephen wrapped his free hand around Christian's throat, tilting Christian's head just so, Christian could tell he was enjoying it just as much.

He shifted his legs, wriggling them back and forth until Stephen's weight settled between them and he could wrap them around Stephen's waist. Christian dug his heels into Stephen's ass, pressing Stephen down, wanting as much skin to skin contact as he could get.

Stephen broke the kiss and moved down to nuzzle at Christian's neck, and Christian smiled as he felt Stephen's hot cock move against his skin, leaving a wet trail behind. It wouldn't be long now. The grip on his throat disappeared and fingers trailed down his skin, ghosting over his abdomen to grab onto his hip.

Lips found his collarbone, and Christian struggled against Stephen's hold again, itching to bury his hands in Stephen's hair, to hold Stephen in place. "Wanna touch you," he rasped out, thrusting up against Stephen.

Brown eyes met his as Stephen pulled back to look at him.

"You don't have to hold me down for me to submit to you. I mean, I like that and all, but I wanna touch, *need* to touch you, bury my hands in your hair, caress your skin, scratch my nails down your back."

The look in Stephen's eyes turned primal, and he released Christian's wrists. "Touch me all you wish, but not your cock. That's mine."

"Okay." Christian nodded, bringing his hands down and threading them through Stephen's thick, curly hair.

Stephen rewarded Christian by sucking a nipple into his mouth, biting it gently and then soothing away the sting with his tongue. Christian held Stephen's head to his chest, wanting more, but Stephen switched sides, giving his other nipple the same treatment. Then he was licking down Christian's chest again, pressing on the marks with his tongue, sending little tiny jolts of pain *pleasure* through Christian's body.

When he reached Christian's cock, Stephen blew over it lightly, nudging it with his nose, until finally Christian let go of his resolve and started to beg. "Please, holy gods, Stephen, just please."

Warm, wet heat engulfed Christian's cock and he would have jerked off the bed with the pleasure of it, except Stephen had the foresight to hold him down, a firm hand pressing on his hip. So Christian could do nothing except lie there and take the pleasure Stephen was giving him.

He whined out loud when Stephen pulled off right before he'd reached the point of no return. Stephen grinned up at him darkly. "If we're gonna mate, we're gonna do it the right way, which means you don't come until I'm inside you."

"What the fuck ever. Just do it already," Christian growled, thrusting his hips up at Stephen. "Hurry up," he whined.

A mischievous chuckle filled the air. "Don't worry, pretty, I'm about to link us together forever."

Christian shuddered at the Alpha timbre in Stephen's voice. "Do it," he gasped out, clutching at Stephen's hips.

He could feel the blunt head of Stephen's cock rubbing over his entrance. Christian pushed against it, trying to pull Stephen in by sheer force of will. But Stephen's hands held tightly onto his hips.

"No, you're not ready. My way; c'mon baby, submit."

Part of Christian rebelled at the order, but his wolf overrode any other instinct, and he found himself spreading his legs wantonly, inviting Stephen to do as he pleased.

"That's it," Stephen crooned, kissing Christian's temple and stroking his face. "So good for me. We're gonna be so good together. No one will be able to stand against us. I'm sure of it."

Christian preened at the praise, bucking up into Stephen's touch and sucking hard on the skin of his shoulder, marking him, *claiming him* as Christian's own. Stephen's hands held on to Christian's head, holding him in place as Christian marked him. "Yes," he cried out in pleasure, rutting against Christian.

Hungrily, Christian licked at Stephen's shoulder, pushing Stephen over onto his back, moving down his chest and marking his collarbone, his need to possess almost as strong as Stephen's seemed to be. Christian dug his fingers into Stephen's sides, keeping Stephen still as Christian licked up and down his chest.

A laugh rumbled through Stephen as his hand combed through Christian's hair. "I know what you're doing."

Looking up at him, Christian cocked an eyebrow.

"And what is that?"

"Making me smell like you."

Then Stephen released a possessive growl, and all talking was finished. Stephen rolled Christian back underneath him. He laced their fingers together and brought them over Christian's head. "By the time we're done, we're both gonna smell like each other."

The kiss was brutal this time, teeth clashing, tongues thrusting hard against each other as Stephen rutted against Christian, leaving a trail of pre-come on his skin. Christian could feel the liquid getting thicker and *more*, and his heart pounded a bit when he remembered why. Stephen let go of his hand and grappled at the drawer in the bedside table, looking for the lube. There'd be no condoms. Werewolves didn't need them. They weren't at risk for normal human diseases. Plus, as Alpha Prime, Stephen instinctively needed to mark his mate, inside and out.

Christian's breath caught in his throat when he felt a cold, lubed finger at his entrance. "Yeah, just fucking yeah."

He pushed down onto Stephen's finger, which quickly turned into two.

"Gods, you are so beautiful, stretched out around my fingers, taking them so beautifully."

"Wanna take your knot," Christian gasped out, rutting on Stephen's fingers.

Two fingers hurriedly became four, and Christian dug his nails into Stephen's skin, eliciting a howl from Stephen. The smell of blood permeated the air, and Christian knew it would happen again before they were finished. Stephen pumped his fingers in and out of Christian until Christian reached down and grabbed his wrist. "Enough," he groaned. "Fuck me, now."

"Just want you to be ready," Stephen said softly,

kissing his jaw again.

"I'm ready. Do it already."

And then the head of Stephen's cock was pushing at his hole, and the burning stretch was so right, Christian had to bite his lip to keep from coming.

"That's it, baby, don't come yet. I'm not even inside you."

Stephen stopped moving, waiting for Christian to nod his head before pushing forward again until all but the Alpha knot at the base of his cock was inside Christian's body. Christian's eyes were shut tight as he willed his body back under control. Stephen's cock was rubbing right over his prostate and just the slightest movement made it feel like he was going to come. His nerves sparked and pleasure rippled up and down his spine, but it wasn't enough. He gripped Stephen's upper arm, his blunt nails digging into the skin again. "Move," he ordered tersely.

Rocking his hips forward, Stephen thrust a little bit farther in before pulling almost all the way out and slamming back into Christian again. His body tightened around Stephen, his muscles just starting to feel that satisfying burn around Stephen's girth. Stephen set up a punishing rhythm, and Christian was crying out with each stroke. Words like *yes, please, more, harder,* and *never stop.*

It seemed to drive Stephen on because he dropped down to whisper his own words in Christian's ear. Words like *love, mine, forever,* and *not going to.* Their movements synced up with those words as Christian finally gave over his last vestige of control, letting his wolf have its way and completely submitting to Stephen.

The emotion of that overwhelmed Christian, and he clung to Stephen, kissing Stephen like he never wanted to be separated from his mate again. Stephen thrust his tongue into Christian's mouth, smoothed some wayward hairs off his forehead, and slowly started to push his knot into Christian's body. The satisfying burn from earlier intensified as Christian felt his muscles stretch more than he'd thought they ever could. He clutched Stephen's hands, squeezing as hard as he possibly could as Stephen pushed farther into him. Christian gasped into Stephen's mouth, and Stephen shushed him. "Take it, baby, come on, I know you can take it for me. You're my mate. Your body was made to do this. Just let go and let it happen. I love you so much; you're doing so well."

Stephen's eyes opened, and Christian stared into them, a million things passing between them. Christian could see desire, hunger, possession, all mixed together with tenderness and love. He could only hope Stephen was seeing the same thing in his eyes because he felt all of it and more as Stephen finally bottomed out and Christian's body adjusted to the size and feel of Stephen's cock inside him. Christian felt like he was being split open as his hole clenched uselessly around Stephen's knot. Inside him, it rested right on his prostate, the constant pressure sending waves of pleasure through his body, overwhelming the burn of being stretched so wide.

"Fuck." Stephen dropped his head down onto Christian's shoulder, breathing hard.

Christian stroked his hands up and down Stephen's back, soothing him, trying to relax Stephen's taut muscles, knowing the effort Stephen was putting out to keep from pounding into him. He turned his head to the side and kissed Stephen on the cheek before whispering in his ear, "It's okay. Do what you need to do. I'm not going to break. You're my mate now. Take what you need."

Pulling back, Stephen looked at Christian, concern on his face, and Christian just cupped his cheek. "I'll be okay, I promise. Now fuck me," he demanded.

The softly spoken words coupled with Christian's

order broke the final bit of control Stephen had. Christian watched as his eyes swirled black and braced himself. "That's it, baby, let go."

And Stephen did. He rocked into Christian, unable to pull out now because the knot at the base of his cock was starting to expand. Christian could feel it growing larger, feel it pulsing over his prostate, knew Stephen was close. It made his own pleasure coil at the base of his spine and spread outward. His cock started to twitch, and he needed to touch, to stroke, anything to get the friction he needed. He wriggled a hand between their bodies to wrap around his cock, but Stephen grabbed his wrist.

"Mine," he growled, firmly pulling Christian's hand away and letting it go. Stephen worked his own hand between their bodies and grabbed Christian's cock, his long fingers squeezing it just right.

"Fuck, yes, please," Christian sighed, his neck arching back as he thrust up into Stephen's fist. Stephen continued thrusting into him, rubbing over his prostate, and Christian could feel his nerves tingling, knew his orgasm wasn't far off. He rocked harder against Stephen, grinding into Stephen's fist and back onto Stephen's cock, actively chasing his orgasm.

Stephen's mouth met his as they kissed, tongues tangling against each other. Christian gripped the back of Stephen's neck, digging in with his nails and drawing blood again, just as Stephen's nails drew blood on his hip. The slight shock of pain, the feel of his mate's hand wrapped around his cock with the perfect amount of pressure, and the burning stretch Christian still felt around Stephen's cock all combined with one final stroke over his prostate to send pleasure exploding through his body.

Christian came with a roar, spurting his come between them, Stephen's thumb pressing into his slit while his cock with its Alpha knot linked them together. Christian sank his teeth into Stephen's shoulder, biting right through the skin, the coppery taste of blood flooding his mouth. He could feel his body tighten around Stephen's knot, milking it, and then Stephen was coming as well, shuddering in his arms, crying out his name. He could almost feel Stephen's warm seed coating his insides, marking him forever.

Stephen's shoulder still caught in his teeth, Christian loosened his grip on Stephen's neck, only to tighten it again when he felt Stephen's knot expand.

"We're mated now, baby, just relax. I'm gonna move again, slowly."

And Stephen rocked into him, brushing over too sensitive areas, pulling moans out of him as he clung to Stephen. Their bodies were locked together, Stephen's knot continuing to expand until Christian was crying out with the *pain* pleasure of it. That's when Stephen struck, sinking his teeth into the side of Christian's neck, drawing blood, marking him forever. Christian held his head in place, the white hot pain of the bite warring with the simple pleasure of finally bonding with his mate until Stephen pulled off and licked at the wound.

Brushing a few strands of hair off Christian's forehead, Stephen looked down at him. "You're mine now, all mine. You did so well."

"How long?" Christian cried out, breathlessly.

Stephen bent down and kissed him softly on the lips. "Not long now. Are you okay?"

Christian nodded, his body feeling too full and yet not full enough. He lifted his legs again, wrapping them around Stephen, digging his heels in, trying to pull Stephen closer. "I want more and yet want it out of me at the same time, how fucked up is that?" He laughed, a bit of a hysterical edge to it.

Kisses rained down on his face as Stephen praised him and reassured him that it wouldn't be like this every time and that the first time was always the worst or so he'd been told by his mother. They rocked slowly together; Christian gave in to his wolf and went pliant in Stephen's arms, just feeling. It was like nothing he'd ever experienced before. Not quite pain, but not overwhelming pleasure, either. Just a connection more intimate than he'd ever expected to have with anyone.

He reveled in the fact that Stephen was literally locking their bodies together, that his mate, the Alpha Prime, had marked him inside and out, branding him forever. He would forever smell like Stephen, and Stephen would always smell like home to him.

"It's ending," Stephen said softly.

The knot inside him was growing smaller; Christian could feel it. He clung to Stephen's shoulders, already mourning the loss of it. A lump of emotion welled up in his throat, and he swallowed hard over it, wondering if it would feel like that every time they finished mating. Stephen started to pull out, and Christian whispered, "Don't."

Stephen kissed the side of his head. "Okay, we'll stay like this for a few more minutes."

They lay in each other's arms until Stephen's cock slipped out of Christian's body on its own. Stephen kissed him then, softly on the lips, tongue teasing and caressing before retreating as the kiss ended. "I need to take a look at you, baby. Make sure you're okay."

Christian nodded, a flush creeping up his body. Stephen kissed his way down Christian's chest before parting Christian's legs. A finger stroked softly over his abused entrance before a soft pair of lips kissed him there. A shudder raced through Christian as Stephen licked him gently and then kissed his inner thigh.

"I'll be right back."

He returned with a warm, wet cloth and talked to

Christian as he cleaned up. Christian tensed as Stephen parted his cheeks and went to wipe over his entrance. But the pain he was expecting was absent, and he looked at Stephen in confusion.

"One of the perks of being Alpha Prime—my saliva has healing properties in it. It's why I'll always insist on licking you clean, so I can heal any damage our mating might have caused. You may still feel some discomfort afterwards, but you will never be injured, not if I can prevent it."

Stephen wiped down Christian's thighs. "We'll have to go back down to the ball, make an appearance, although I'm sure a lot of people have figured things out by now. It's almost midnight, time for the big reveal. We've been gone a long time."

"What about that guy? You know, the one on the Council, the one you said was trying to make you into something you aren't?"

"No worries, he won't be on the Council for long. Not once I've introduced you as my Mate--" Stephen paused for a moment, looking at Christian with uncertainty in his eyes. "What are your parents going to think about this?"

His brow furrowed, Christian thought for a moment and then gave Stephen a reassuring smile. "As long as I'm happy, they'll be happy and support whatever we do."

Relief flooded Stephen's face. "Well, then, with your family's support and approval, I should have all the backing I need to get rid of him and anyone else on the Council who feels the same way he does."

He kissed the top of Christian's head. "Come on. Let's get cleaned up, redressed, and back down to the ball. I'm anxious to show you off to everyone and to start the next chapter."

Christian rolled his eyes and laughed, but let himself

be tugged into the bathroom. The shower took longer than necessary because Stephen was very thorough in cleaning them both. Christian made himself a mental note to ask about that later, not that he minded, just found it amusing. He wondered if Stephen would do the same when they were in wolf form. They dressed quickly, Christian helping Stephen get his bow tie properly tied and straight.

Standing side by side, looking at their reflections in the full-length mirror, Christian couldn't help but notice the contrast. "Light and dark," he said reverently.

Stephen raked his eyes over their reflections and turned to him. "Fitting though, isn't it? We complement each other, just the way mates are supposed to." He turned back to the mirror and slid an arm around Christian's waist. "Come on, time to go."

They walked toward the door, and Christian bent to pick his mask off the floor, intending to slip it on when Stephen stopped him.

"No. No more masks, not for each other and not for them. We go out there together, a united front, as ourselves."

Without saying a word, Christian set the mask down on the chair by the door, took Stephen's hand and nodded. Together, they walked hand in hand down the stairs, through the house, reaching the entrance of the ballroom just as the count to midnight reached zero. Masks were taken off, and heads turned to see the two of them standing on the threshold.

A spotlight found its way over them, making Christian blink and hold up a hand to deflect the glare. Stephen cleared his throat and squeezed Christian's hand a bit tighter.

"Thank you all for coming tonight. I hope you've had a good time, made some new friends, reconnected with old ones. But most of all, I hope you've been able to be yourselves. There's a certain freedom that comes with being able to hide behind a mask, in being able to 'come as you aren't' so to speak. That's why the announcements were done away with, so you could mingle and converse with as much anonymity as possible. It's the first of many changes I hope to make as Alpha Prime."

Stephen paused and turned to look at Christian, smiling at him before turning back to the crowd. "The first official thing I'd like to do is introduce you to my Beta Prime, Christian Thomas. I'm sure a lot of you know him and his family."

As Christian watched, a sheepish look appeared on Stephen's face.

"We uh, didn't get a chance to tell them about this. It just sort of happened and here we are."

His grip on Christian's hand tightened, and Christian glanced over to see his parents moving through the crowd toward them. When they were within hearing distance, Christian's father raised his glass.

"I offer a toast, to the Alpha Prime and the Beta Prime. Long may you live in happiness, love, and success."

"Here Here!" A chorus of voices rang out through the ballroom as glasses were raised in their honor.

A lump of emotion grew in Christian's throat as he looked at his mom and dad. His mom was smiling and crying at the same time, and his dad mouthed the words, "I'm proud of you."

But then he saw Cherry waving and practically bursting with happiness right behind them and had to suppress a laugh at her unbridled enthusiasm.

When the applause subsided, Stephen spoke again. "Now, relax, drink, and enjoy the party. The night is still young!"

He turned around with Christian in tow and went back

out into the foyer. He pulled Christian to him, wrapped his arms around Christian and sighed.

Christian could feel the tension leaking out of him and kissed the side of Stephen's neck, a few scant inches away from the bite mark he'd left. "Told you it'd be okay."

Stephen tightened the hug, and Christian smiled before pulling out of it reluctantly. "Come on, you have a pack to run and a Beta to show off."

"This is only the start you know," Stephen said softly, trailing a finger down Christian's face. "It's not going to be easy."

"Them?"

"Them and us."

"Nah, the us will be the easy part, because at the end of the day you're still Wolfsbane15 and I'm still DocWolf24. That's who we are underneath it all. We just have to get used to the outer packaging. If we remember that, well, things have a way of working themselves out for the best."

Stephen smiled and leaned down, kissing him gently on the lips. "Let's go change our world."

Holding hands, they went back to the ballroom where they were immediately surrounded by Pack members who wanted to congratulate them. And as they accepted all the accolades, Christian held tightly to Stephen's hand. He knew change wouldn't be easy, it never was. He and Stephen still had to talk, but that would come later, long after the guests were gone. Stephen turned to him and caught his eye, smiling at him, squeezing his hand. Christian returned the smile, trusting that the bond they'd formed not even an hour earlier would carry them through whatever lay ahead.

Masks Off!

What You Are
by Elizabeth L. Brooks

Cory pushed the "up" button and stepped back to wait, wondering yet again what idiot had designed the twenty-six story building with only two elevators, both of them as slow as molasses. Naturally, both cars were high up in the 20s. Cory began to read the fliers and advertisements pinned to the building's bulletin board and taped to the wall around it: blood drive next month, a few lost-and-found notices, a couple of exercise groups, adverts for local eateries with photocopied menus in their takeaway pockets, local events that might attract an audience here. The word "shifter" caught Cory's eye, and he scanned the parts of the poster that hadn't been covered with other things: it was for a support group for the families and friends of shifters. Cory snorted at the wording ("even co-workers and colleagues") that subtly but unmistakably implied that no one who worked in such a high-class building could actually *be* a shifter.

"We meet again!" That voice was deep and dark, with just a hint of roughness to it that made Cory's stomach flop and his cock twitch. Leon Conwy pulled up beside Cory, as he did at least three mornings each week—Leon's bus route apparently coincided almost exactly with Cory's train—and absently checked the elevator bank to see how much of a wait remained. "How was your weekend?"

"Spent most of it working on a big project; you know how it is. How about you?" Cory schooled his expression into what he hoped was friendly interest and not desperate lust. Big city or not, the habit of secrecy was too well-ingrained in Cory for him to make the first move, and if Leon was interested in Cory beyond the chats they had on the elevator several mornings a week, nothing had been said. To be honest, Cory didn't know what he would do if Leon *did* indicate any interest in him—the firm he worked for was staunchly conservative, and he was positive that coming out as gay would significantly damage his career there.

Leon grinned. "Took my niece and nephew camping," he said. "It was great. Nothing around us but the lake and the trees and the sky. It was even warm enough to do without the tent."

Cory smiled, half-envious, half-frightened. "I've never been camping," he confessed. He'd never dared. Camping would require being outdoors after dark.

"Oh, you should try it!" Leon said. "There's nothing like it!"

"Mm." Cory grabbed a card from the holder advertising a masquerade charity ball a few weeks away. "This is more my speed, really."

"Yeah?" Leon reached for a card of his own. Cory had to hold his breath against Leon's rich scent, a perfect match to that whiskey-dark voice. Leon finished reading the card, then shrugged and put it back. "I wouldn't even know where to get a mask."

"Oh, I found a little shop over on 18th that has all kinds of stuff like that," Cory said. He hadn't been looking for masks at the time, just exploring the city he'd been living in for only a few months, but the store had drawn him in with its fascinating and eclectic selections. The masks had covered half a wall, gorgeous confections decorated with gems and feathers and ribbons. He'd almost bought one shaped like a wolf's head, but it was too beautiful and expensive to waste on such a bitter jest.

The elevator finally dinged its arrival, and they got on. Cory pressed the 16 for himself, and the 14 for Leon.

"But really, you should give camping a try sometime," Leon pressed. "Maybe I could set something up."

Craig's fingers tingled, his whole body zinging with desire. Was that an invitation? A come-on? It didn't matter; Craig had too many secrets to keep. But still, to be alone with Leon, far away from the city and anyone who might see them... It would take careful planning to arrange such a trip for a weekend with no moon. "Eh, maybe," he said noncommittally. "My schedule gets pretty crazy."

"Sure, sure," Leon said easily. "But let me know, okay?"

"You bet," Cory said.

When lunchtime rolled around, Cory went outside to the vendor who parked his cart across the street from the office building. He bought two hot dogs with sauerkraut and onions—*no one to kiss, might as well*—and sat on a bench to enjoy them. Sometimes he saw Leon again when the other man came out to take his own lunch, but not today, apparently.

As he tucked his wallet back into his pocket, he encountered the charity masquerade advert card. He took it out and looked at it again. The illustration was a stylized image of a woman in a long, flowing dress with a feathered mask over her face; the feathers of the mask and the billowing hem of her dress curled out and up to become a frame around the words. The ball was next month, on the new moon, as it happened. Cory blinked as he realized that, and wondered if he should go. His supervisor was always pressing him for details of how he was settling in after his move, and Cory had realized just recently that the man was fishing for signs that Cory had a social life outside of work, some balance against the long hours Cory put in that would make him less of a risk for burnout.

Cory double-checked the date against the calendar that always seemed emblazoned in fire in his mind. No moon that night. No danger of revealing his darker secret. It would give him an excuse to go back to that little shop on 18th. He even knew how to dance, having taken a ballroom course in college to help out a friend who needed a partner. If only he could dance with the men instead of women, feel strong arms surrounding him and give himself over to their guidance...

An idea sparked to life, and Cory smiled as he tucked the card back into his pocket and stood up. He'd have to finish his work quickly, and then he'd need to start shopping.

Cory took a taxi from his apartment building to the civic center where the ball was being held. The taxi driver seemed not at all perturbed by Cory's appearance, though he'd slaved for hours on the elaborate getup.

He'd scoured store after boutique after hole-in-the-wall consignment to find the perfect dress, and had finally found it in a tiny bridal shop. It was a blood-red satin with inset gores and decorative piping of silvery grey. The crosslaced waist fell into a flared skirt that stopped less than a centimeter above the pavement when he was wearing the designer-knockoff sandals he'd bought to go with it. Its high neck covered his Adam's apple, but the open back and sleeveless arms showed off his smooth, pale skin. He'd doubted his own sanity when he'd realized he would have to buy a backless bra and falsies to wear under it—in a city this size, there were surely stores that catered to his needs, but he had no idea where to find them or how to go about looking, since he hadn't done any crossdressing since college, and even then it had been no more than a fun lark to make his female friends laugh. But the internet was his salvation, and the B cups he'd chosen fit perfectly, being small enough not to be easily dislodged but big enough to allay suspicion over the breadth of his chest. It was a good thing that he was naturally slender.

He'd told the woman at the wig shop that it was for his twin sister, who was in chemo. He wasn't sure she'd bought the story, but she hadn't balked at fitting the wig to his own scalp. Its glorious black ringlets were arranged like a storybook princess', covering his own unremarkable chestnut brown.

Over his face, he wore a mask, of course. It had cost as much as the entire rest of his costume, but he'd paid it gladly. The face was shaped like an eagle's, white and gray, a swirl of silver sparkles at the temples to highlight the eyes. The beak that covered his nose and curved down to hide his mouth (while still letting him slip food and even a glass underneath, if he wished) was brilliantly yellow, accented with what seemed a hundred different colors. Around the sides, hiding the elastic and ribbons that held it on, were real eagle feathers: small, downy ones against his face and enormous pinfeathers, beautiful in their natural browns and grays and whites, standing out around the edges.

It had been gorgeous hanging on the wall, but when he'd put it on and looked into the mirror, it had come alive. So perfect and disturbing was the illusion of life, despite the abstract decorative designs, that Cory had nearly panicked and pulled it off again. But as he looked, his heart pounding, he had realized that proud eagle with the gray eyes so like his own was someone who could dare things that secret-laden Cory never would. It was someone he needed to be, if only for one evening.

The masquerade was surprisingly well-attended, the ballroom a bright throng after the subdued darkness of the summer night. Cory emerged from the taxi, glanced reflexively at the sky, and then stood for a long moment on the sidewalk outside, looking through the open doors into the crowd of color and fabric beyond as he collected himself.

You can do this. It had been a year or more since he'd dressed in drag, but he'd had a knack for it right from the start, when a few college friends had talked him into trying out for a part in a crossgendered Shakespearean production and he'd landed the part of Lady Macbeth. *Forget that thing between your legs: you're a woman. A beautiful, seductive woman, strong and confident. A huntress.* Cory felt his arms and shoulders settle into a new posture, felt his hips swaying against the luxurious glide of the dress fabric, and he—no, *she*—climbed the steps to where the ticket takers were waiting.

Within, the music pulled him forward into the crowd, and he smiled under the mask as the crowd parted, men and women alike turning to stare. He didn't dare speak—Cory's voice wasn't as deep as Leon's, but would still give him away instantly—but he nodded elegantly to those who spoke in greeting.

"May I have this dance?" The voice was dark like

Leon's, but rougher. Cory turned to find himself eye-to-eye with a man wearing the face of a white leopard, nearly as beautiful as Cory's own mask, over the simple elegance of a tuxedo. Broad shoulders filled the suit's timeless elegance well, and the deep brown eyes behind the mask had a hunger that made Cory's body tingle. He took the offered hand and followed the leopard onto the dance floor.

The leopard danced well, not with the intuition of a long-time partner, but with knowledge and grace. He signaled his intended movements to Cory with subtle shifts and pressures that let them sweep across the floor with style that turned heads. "You can actually dance!" The leopard let out an actual purr of delight as Cory responded appropriately to his cues. He spun Cory out into the floor, making the red and silver satin flare and swirl, and then drew Cory inexorably back against the leopard's chest, their masks all but kissing. "Promise you'll find me again if they play a rhumba."

Cory was wordless, but not without answer. He tipped his head sideways, as if considering, then nodded once, solemn.

He might not have bothered, though. The very next song offered up the rhumba's lilting strains, and the leopard squeezed Cory's hand as his other hand settled on Cory's hip. "It must be fate," the leopard quipped, and though Cory tossed his head disdainfully, he was grateful the mask hid his blush. "The dance of love," Cory's dance instructor had told them, and so Cory threw himself into the role with abandon, letting his body flirt shamelessly with the leopard as they circled one another and waited for the music to bring them to the consummation of their musical passion. It was exhilarating.

As the night wore on, the leopard rarely left Cory's side. He didn't seem to mind that Cory couldn't talk, didn't seem obliged to fill every moment with his own chatter. They suited well as dance partners, though as the man began to press closer and closer, it became harder and harder for Cory to keep the erection hidden under his dress a secret.

Finally, he feigned exhaustion and left the dance floor entirely. Following a thread of cooler air, he found himself pushing through a curtain onto a balcony. Gratefully, Cory leaned on the railing.

Arms slid around his waist and a firm body pressed against his, a hard cock unmistakable against Cory's hip. The leopard had followed. Cory hesitated, but the leopard's hand was stroking the satin against his stomach. It felt good, so good... It couldn't end well, he knew, but Cory couldn't resist a few moments of illusion. He sighed and pressed back against the leopard's lean, hard form.

The leopard chuckled. There was a moment of hesitation, a soft rustle, and lips pressed, ever so lightly, to the spot just behind Cory's ear. Cory had only a startled instant in which to realize the leopard had unmasked before the hand on his stomach moved with more urgency and the leopard's other hand began to trace the rim of Cory's ear, ruffling the eagle feathers there. His lips brushed Cory's ear, and he whispered, "I know what you are."

Cory froze. What did that mean? Who was this man, and what did he think he knew about Cory? It could have been a simple flirtation, but Cory could not risk that chance. He pushed away with sudden force and fled, gracelessly dodging the other masqueraders in his blind flight for the door. It didn't occur to him to look back until he was nearly out on the street. No one appeared to be chasing him, but Cory did not stop.

It wasn't until Cory had stumbled into his apartment and locked the door that he thought to take off his mask.

Three long feathers had gone missing from just over his ear. Cory shuddered with animal panic. He put the mask quickly into its box and then stuffed the box under the bed. This was what came, he chided himself, of giving rein to one's forbidden desires. *Your desires are immaterial*, he reminded himself. *Some things are better left hidden and buried.*

It wasn't until Cory was on the train Monday morning that he thought about Leon. Cory hadn't allowed himself the luxury of responding even vaguely to Leon's subtle flirtations (if that was what they even were), but the masquerade had left him flustered, his mental walls damaged and crumbling. What would he say if Leon made another of his gentle suggestions that they meet outside the office building some time? Cory blushed furiously at the mere thought.

He couldn't face Leon like this.

He slowed and then approached the building cautiously, trying to blend in with other commuters. It wasn't easy; Cory's need to avoid moonlight meant that he came in as soon after dawn as he could manage so that he could leave to be home by sunset. There weren't many on this side of town who kept such hours, but after a few minutes, he found another early riser to follow into the building. At least with a third person present, Leon would have to stick to general conversation. But all Cory's machinations were for naught: Leon did not appear.

Nor did he come on Tuesday. Or Wednesday. By Friday, Cory was worried. While it was common for their commutes to fail to sync up occasionally, he'd never gone a whole week without seeing Leon by the elevator bank. As he entered the waiting lift, he found himself glancing back over his shoulder, hoping to see Leon jogging in off the street. "Don't be stupid," he muttered under his breath as he jabbed the 16. "The bus schedule probably changed. Or he's taking a vacation. The man's not obliged to register his plans with you."

Cory fretted as the lethargic machine began its ascent. If he didn't see Leon on Monday, he decided, he would... What? What could he do? Cory didn't know the man's last name, or even where he worked—just that he took the bus and worked on the fourteenth floor. Cory supposed he could go to the offices on the fourteenth and ask around—but he gave up that notion almost immediately as he tried to imagine any possible permutation of such a conversation that would not end in disaster for him.

He was so busy pondering the dilemma that he nearly set his briefcase down on the envelope on his desk. Startled out of his reverie, he picked it up. It was lightweight but not flat. The envelope was a standard interoffice pouch, legal-sized and dull orange, but it obviously hadn't been delivered by the interoffice mail: instead of the white-and-blue IOM address label, it just had "Cory" written across the front in black marker, the letters large and neat. There was nothing else to indicate who had sent it or what it might contain.

Suddenly uneasy, Cory looked around, but there weren't many people in the office yet, and none of them were watching him. Cory unwound the string, hesitated. Finally, he screwed up his courage and dumped the contents out on his desk: a plain white sheet of note paper, folded into quarters, and an eagle's feather.

Cory swallowed hard and picked up the feather. Down near the base, glue and glitter still clung.

"I know what you are," the leopard whispered in his memory, puffs of breath against his ear simultaneously arousing and chilling. He had known Cory wasn't a woman. He had known *exactly* who Cory was. He knew, or had guessed, that Cory was gay.

What else did he know? Cory's hand shook so hard as he picked up the note that it took him three tries to unfold it.

"I didn't mean to frighten you. I hoped I'd see you at the unmasking so I could apologize and explain, but you were gone. If you will meet me at the Black Street entrance to Luwy Park at 6:00 tonight, I would love to make it up to you. If you choose not to come, please know that I'm sorry." It was unsigned and had been written in the same strong, neat hand that had printed his name on the envelope.

Cory read the note again. It didn't read like an obsessed stalker to him. But Luwy Park? At six?

Cory could do it, despite the moon's return to the sky; it wouldn't be dark until after eight. He would simply have to keep the conversation short. *Or take him home with me.* Cory shushed that thought; it threatened his defenses and facades on every front.

Should he go? He wanted to confront the man who had thrown him for such a loop, but would he risk exposing himself to do it? And what if he was wrong about the note's polite tone—what if it really was some kind of crazy stalker?

But if it was a stalker, Cory would only have to wait for moonrise, wouldn't he? Learning that the object of your obsession was a shifter was bound to cool even the hottest flame. Cory laughed mirthlessly to himself.

Of course, if the stalker already *knew* Cory was a shifter (*I know what you are*) then seeing the change was more likely to be encouragement than a deterrent.

But the note was so effacing and polite and deferential! Cory could call the police, but they would want to know all the details, and when they found out he was a shifter, and a gay one at that, he didn't think they'd be much help.

Cory looked down at his desk and realized he'd been sitting there, twirling the eagle feather in his fingers and letting his thoughts chase their own tail for hours. The clock said 4:00, and he hadn't even made a pretense of work since before lunch.

He had to know, Cory realized, or this wondering would drive him mad. Decision abruptly made, Cory closed his laptop and began to pack his things. He would go to the park early and watch the entrance. Surely, he would recognize the man on approach, and he could decide then whether to reveal himself.

The late afternoon sun was glorious, its heat a nearly solid presence on Cory's shoulders. He stood in a leafy alcove from which he could see the Black Street entrance without being immediately visible himself. In the first hour of his watch, he'd seen a lot of pretty, younger women walking with dogs and children—in this upper-class area, he expected they were nannies exercising their charges. There were a few gaggles of teenagers, and then the retirees who inhabited the park during the days began their resigned shuffle homeward. As the working day drew to a close, the number of professionals sharply increased, men and women alike dressed in power suits and carrying leather briefcases as they cut through the park to get to the subway and train stops on the far side.

Cory watched more closely now as the appointed hour drew nigh, hoping to spot someone he recognized. His gaze weighed every man, mentally fitting each into a tuxedo, his ears straining to hear the voices that continued to do business over their cell phones.

"I might've known you'd come early."

Cory nearly jumped out of his skin as the low rumble came from only inches away. He spun around, hand lifting in automatic ward--

Leon. He was close enough to kiss, though his expression was grave, neither playful nor seductive. He had another of Cory's mask feathers tucked into his suit's breast pocket, apparently by way of identification. Cory swallowed and suddenly felt ashamed: how could he not have recognized the man he'd been fantasizing about for months? How could he have misheard that voice?

Suddenly aware that he was standing with his mouth agape, Cory closed it with a snap. Leon tipped his head slightly. "You really didn't know it was me," he said, and that was surprise in his voice. He withdrew a half-step.

Cory felt heat climb his neck. "I didn't. I guess I should have, but--" He tried to search for words that would explain how he had been someone else that night, someone who gave boring, staid Cory's acquaintances barely a thought. But no words would come. Or at least, none that weren't even more insulting or hurtful. Another thought occurred. "You thought I did know. That I was, what? Playing a game?"

Leon smiled then, and Cory was not imagining the hint of guilt there. "I did. It was a rude assumption, I know."

"You weren't wrong," Cory said. "But it wasn't the game you thought." He grimaced. "I can't believe I didn't recognize you," he groaned. "And despite my... my costume, you knew me."

Leon's smile melted into a grimace of chagrin. "And that means you were truly frightened, not merely startled, when I said I knew you. I'm more sorry than I can begin to express. I didn't mean to threaten you, I promise."

Cory swallowed hard, nodded. "I know." He drew a shuddering breath, then another, more steady. "I know.

It's all right. What's done is done." He glanced up at the sky. The blue was beginning to slant toward purple, and on a Friday evening, his commute home could take over an hour. "I should be going. I'll see you next week?" He forced a quick, casual smile as he stepped sideways to leave the alcove.

Leon caught his arm and drew him back. "Going? Now that we've finally stopped dancing around the question?" The smile was back, warm and very much seductive now. "I did promise to make it up to you."

Cory shook his head. "I can't. I-- I want to." Even that admission made his carefully-honed mental censor shriek. "I'm sorry. I really am. But I can't. If anyone found out--"

Leon drew him deeper into the alcove, and though Cory knew he should pull away, he let it happen. "I know," Leon rumbled. That voice, that *voice*. It resonated deep in Cory's belly, made him want to howl. "I can be discreet," Leon promised. "Strictly hands-off in public, the works. But stay with me tonight. This whole week, staying away from you..."

Cory closed his eyes and set his feet. "I *can't*, Leon. There's more to it than being in the closet."

"What else?" Leon's voice came from very close; Cory could feel warm breath on his face.

Cory shook his head. "Don't ask."

"At least have dinner with me. Let me show you. I won't even ask for a kiss goodnight."

Cory wanted badly to give in and absolutely dared not. He glared at Leon instead, letting the frustration morph into anger. "I said no!"

Startled, Leon released him, and Cory's arm felt cold. "You're right." Leon's eyes closed as he drew and released a slow breath. "Will you at least give me a hint? I'll admit, I'm hurting. I want a reason to hang it on."

God, the last thing Cory wanted was for Leon to feel

wounded and rejected. But shame weighted the words and would not let them loose from his throat. Finally, his eyes sliding to the blank wall of vegetation, he stammered, "I need to be home before dark." That was clear enough, wasn't it? He took two quick steps back; he'd heard of too many violent responses not to want a head start if he was going to need a quick escape.

No one wanted to have anything to do with shifters, not in Cory's experience. Never mind that it was a genetic mutation, not communicable, or that scientific studies showed that shifted folk weren't particularly violent. Those storybook prejudices were rooted deep in people's consciousness and hard to overcome. At least Cory's parents hadn't turned him out when his condition had manifested. They'd helped him excuse his way around nighttime activities and brought to him every far-fetched article that tried to explain the sudden appearance of the shifter mutation (biogenetic research gone wrong? leakage from nuclear power plants? extraterrestrial tampering? subtle enemy contagion? punishment from God?); they insisted he attempt every pseudo-scientific treatment that provided even a hope of reversing it. Family was important to them, and they'd stood by him, in their way. But they'd withdrawn as well, suddenly turning the full force of their hopes and dreams on Cory's younger siblings.

Feeling abandoned, Cory had told his best friend, Don. Don had promptly distanced himself from Cory, though in a sort of memorial to a decade of friendship, he'd at least kept the secret, letting their parents and other friends believe it was a falling out over a girl. Cory, at fourteen, hadn't even figured out yet that he was gay.

He'd spent the next four years as a loner, quietly plotting his escape. By the time Cory's sexuality made itself clear, he kept it to himself, knowing it was just one more thing that would hurt his parents and earn him ridicule if it came out. He'd applied himself furiously to his studies (what else could he do with his evenings, when he couldn't join his classmates on the sports field or at parties that might spill out of doors?) and earned a full scholarship to college.

At college, he'd done much the same. It had been like a breath of fresh air to know there was no one there who might spill his secrets. He couldn't imagine walking willingly back into that situation, and so he'd avoided the campus LGBT union and refused to even look at the fliers for shifter support groups. Let others agitate for equality; let others seek open acceptance. Cory wanted only to pass for the quiet and bookish student they thought him to be. His penchant for theater was enough of an oddity without adding less socially-acceptable traits to the mix.

After school, he'd deliberately taken a job in the most conservative firm he could, knowing they'd never willingly hire shifters or gays—not as a subversive act of rebellion, but to assure himself that he wouldn't be faced with others who shared his secrets. And now, in retribution for one evening of abandon, his carefully-constructed walls of safety were crashing down.

It occurred to him that Leon hadn't responded to his revelation. He braced himself for ugliness—disgust, fear, betrayal—and looked at Leon.

Leon wasn't showing any of those. Instead, he looked mildly confused. He was simply looking at Cory, as if he was waiting for the rest, an explanation that would make sense of his words.

Cory swallowed a decade's worth of bile. "I'm a *shifter*," he threw at the other man, angry that he was being forced to use the words.

Leon still looked confused. "I know that," he said slowly. "I could smell it on you from the first time we met. Didn't you--?" His face cleared from confusion into something like horror. "Oh, God, you've never actually shifted, have you? How the *fuck*--" He broke off, shaking his head.

Cory felt like he was being sucked into a maelstrom, a storm whose eye blinked over a land Cory had never even imagined. "You? You're a-- You're one, too?"

"Jesus fucking Christ," Leon said conversationally. He reached across the space between them quickly, before Cory could withdraw farther, taking Cory's hands. "I'm completely fucking this up."

"I don't think I've ever heard you curse before," Cory observed. He felt suddenly distant, removed from himself.

"This is a very special circumstance," Leon grated. He paused, visibly regrouping. "Haven't you ever shifted even once?"

Cory shook his head. "It was part of the medical before high school," he explained numbly. "You know. Vaccinations up to date, growth according to the charts, spine straight, all that. The shifter test came back... inconclusive. I hadn't quite hit puberty yet, is probably why, but they sent a vial of my blood down to the hospital for tests, and when the results came back..." He shrugged.

Leon still had hold of his hands. Cory didn't try to pull free. It felt good, freeing, to finally talk about it, even in a breathless whisper. "My folks didn't freak too badly, but they kept a pretty close watch on me after that. I only got to go out in the rain. Or on the new moon." He looked into Leon's face and found it filled with understanding and concern, and it nearly undid him. He kept talking, the words pouring from him in a sudden violent flood. He talked about Don's abandonment, about his family's tight-lipped care, about discovering the freedom of secrecy and the plan he'd made for himself, and through it all, Leon only listened, though his mouth often twitched as if he was suppressing some comment or question.

167

By the time Cory wound down, it was far too late for him to get home before nightfall. The sky was purple and orange, evening stars visible and growing brighter with each passing breath. Cory bit his lip. "I don't have a cloak or a cover-up here," he groaned. "I'm stuck. Is there a place I can hide in the park?"

Leon frowned, but nodded. "Yeah. We should talk a bit, anyway. Come on." He kept hold of one of Cory's hands and led the way out of the alcove. "I'm not letting go," he said, gentle and firm as if he was soothing a restive animal. "But I promise, no one will see us. This way." He led Cory into the center of the park to the now-abandoned children's playground, and into a steel tube, tall enough for them to crouch or kneel. "Here. The moon's path won't peek past the very opening."

Cory felt ridiculous, crawling into a child's tunnel, but his heart was pounding with panic. Once inside, he shrugged out of his suit jacket and folded it across his lap as he sat on the sandy floor. Leon settled across from him, their folded legs touching. In the swiftly-fading light, it was hard to see Leon's face, but he seemed to be watching Cory intently.

"I'm trying to decide where to begin," Leon admitted finally. "Part of me just wants to find you a shifter-friendly therapist and dump you in their lap."

Cory chuckled mirthlessly. "Don't forget gay-friendly, too."

"That, too. But I feel like I've screwed up so badly, I need to do something to set it right. I don't even... Are you a virgin, too?"

Cory blushed. "Close, but not quite." Another regret. He'd let his guard down once in college and written it off the next day as a drunken exploration rather than anything meaningful, deliberately leaving a broken heart behind rather than risk his precious secrets.

"Well, I guess that's something. Cory, you don't have to keep hiding from the shift, you know."

Cory snorted.

"I'm serious," Leon protested. "It's not a bad thing. It doesn't hurt. You're not going to hurt anyone else. You can't infect anyone with it. It's just a... a change. Like having five o'clock shadow at the end of the day. But hairier."

"Don't forget the tail," Cory said. "You're telling me to give in to this, this *thing* that's invading me!"

"Cory. Cory. Listen to me. Please." Leon took his hand again and squeezed it, hard. "If it's in you, then it's there. It's not going away. You might as well take the advantages that it gives you, right? The sense of smell, the hearing... Once you've made the change, they stick with you. And it's a good feeling, Cory, I swear. If they offered me a cure today, I wouldn't take it."

Cory bit his lip, unable to articulate his fears, but Leon seemed to understand. "Just... Watch me. I'll go first." He released Cory and stood up on his knees, unbuttoning his shirt.

"What are you doing?"

Leon flashed a quick smile. "Lots easier to get out of clothes while I still have thumbs." He loosely folded the shirt and laid it on the sand, unfastened his belt.

Leon's chest was broad and muscular, lightly studded with a soft fur the same color as his hair. Cory's breath suddenly came faster. "Leon, I don't... I'm not sure this is a good idea."

"Maybe not," Leon allowed. "But you should see it, once. Should feel it." He had to rise to his feet, crouching, to bare his feet and kick off his pants and boxers. Despite the awkward position, he moved with grace, and Cory wanted to touch him again. He kept his hands firmly to himself.

Leon caught Cory's eyes. "It will be fine," he promised. He brushed his fingers through Cory's hair and then let his hand fall away again. "Just watch. Join me when you're ready."

"Leon, don't--" It was too late. Leon had left the tunnel. Leon straightened into the weak, silvery light of the crescent moon; from his vantage, Cory could see Leon's long legs and lower back.

Leon shuddered and sighed, then melted into the shape of a large wolf, as swiftly and quietly as a man might put on a coat.

Cory had seen transformations before. He had spent hours watching footage online, dissecting every twitch and movement, trying to track each disparate change. But he'd never seen it in real life. He'd never been so close or felt so emotionally charged. He couldn't restrain a gasp.

Leon—the wolf that was Leon—turned to look at him, and Cory froze. The wolf that was Leon was beautiful, with a rich reddish-brown coat and luminous, yellow eyes. He also had shockingly long teeth. Cory held his breath as the massive creature padded into the tunnel, bringing those long, white teeth ever nearer.

The wolf sneezed, and sneezed again. Before Cory could recover from his startle, Leon's head had wormed under Cory's hand. His fur was just as soft and thick as it looked, and his tongue was now lolling out of the side of his mouth, almost ridiculous. It made it hard to hold on to his fear.

Leon caught Cory's sleeve in his teeth and tugged gently—once, twice, three times. Then he let go and backed out of the tunnel. He trotted a few steps away, then gave Cory an expectant look.

Cory shook his head. "I don't know. I'm just not... I need time to prepare." Could the wolf understand him?

Leon sneezed again and shook all over. He turned and

ran out into the park, out of Cory's line of sight.

"Wait!" Cory called. "Wait, don't-- Damn it." He sat back on the sand.

He was stuck. He could either give in to the moon and the wolf—and it seemed that Leon, at least, had his wolf well under control—or he was stuck in this damned tunnel until sunrise. Cory took a deep breath and began to strip.

He hesitated at the mouth of the tunnel for a long moment. Was this really what he wanted to do? But then he caught sight of the wolf sitting at the far edge of the playground, calmly watching. Waiting for him. Cory swallowed hard and stepped into the moonlight.

No matter what Leon had said, Cory assumed there would be pressure and pain as his bones and muscles rearranged themselves; prickling on his skin as fur grew; mental fogginess as his brain was subsumed by the wolf within.

He had assumed wrong. The change of shape was only a rearrangement of limbs, no less natural-feeling than lying down on his bed at the end of a long day. The sudden growth of hair glided over his skin like the softest of fur coats. And his mind was no more disturbed by the wolf's sudden presence than it would have been by a sudden and vivid memory.

Cory shook himself all over, feeling dusty and restless. His mind was still his own, but the wolf's presence had shaped him somewhat. His priorities felt awkward, his fears strange and unnecessary. Cory took a few steps, amazed (and yet, detached and serene, perfectly accepting) to find that the movement was no stranger, no less normal than walking as a man.

Leon was approaching, coming from upwind so that Cory would not be startled by him. He smelled *amazing*. Cory wanted to bury his nose in Leon's mane and just breathe in the scent, but Leon sidled as he drew close, bumping into Cory's side. Cory stumbled a few steps to keep his balance, and looked at Leon in surprise. Tongue lolling in a grin, Leon nudged him again and then took off running.

Cory didn't even think about that before he was running, too. There was nothing in this run but the simple joy of it: the feel of wind in his fur, the rush and rustle of leaves, the feeling of muscles stretching after long disuse.

The park was not small, but they lapped it several times, dodging in and out of trees, weaving through the bushes that lined the bike paths, racing without trying to win, playing a never-ending game of tag. If he'd been in his human shape, Cory would have been laughing with joy. As it was, he couldn't resist a sharp yelp of triumph when he tackled Leon and they rolled into the dewy grass.

Leon bit playfully at Cory's ruff; Cory twisted loose to close his jaws over Leon's muzzle. Leon shook him off and knocked him over again, and for a time they wrestled, sneezing with laughter. Then Leon's scent changed—became sharper, more serious. Hungrier. Cory broke off his mock-attack in surprise, and Leon bowled him over with more force than before, stood over him, staring. The scent grew stronger, and Cory realized this was a mating-scent, that Leon wanted him.

For an instant, Cory was filled with panic—they were shifted! in a public park!—but the wolf's matter-of-fact approach to life smothered all question of propriety. Cory *did* want Leon, after all, didn't he? What did it matter what shape they were in? Tentatively, Cory lifted his head and licked Leon's muzzle in an approximation of a human kiss.

It was Leon who was startled now, but he recovered quickly. He bit at Cory's neck, a little more sharply this time. Cory's whole body wiggled in anticipation; Leon's musk had enveloped him like a cloud, heightening his own need. His cock had grown out of its sheath, giving off its own unmistakable scent.

Leon *whuff*ed with something Cory suspected was amusement, but his dark head dipped and his long tongue lapped at Cory's cock until Cory let loose a pleading whimper.

A few nudges from Leon got Cory back on his feet, his hind legs braced and his tail curled firmly to the side, exposing his passage. Each second was an eternity. Leon's nose snuffled at Cory's back end, and he nearly yelped with surprise and spilled his seed right there.

But then Leon was on him, covering him, his thick member driving home in Cory's body. A low, soft whine slipped from Cory's throat, but his legs had stiffened to help him push back into their union. Each thrust was a sensation Cory had never dreamed possible, each moment of pleasure better than the last. Leon growled possessively and bit Cory again, marking him, but even that pain was exquisite. At last, Leon surged deep, releasing a soft growl of pleasure, and Cory's own climax swept over him, spattering the grass and leaves with his seed.

Leon nudged Cory back toward the playground. Suddenly sleepy, Cory went without protest. In the dark den of the tunnel, the two wolves curled together. Cory fell asleep within moments and dreamed of running in the moonlight.

Something—someone—was licking his balls. Cory was immediately awake, but it took him a moment longer to piece together his surroundings. He was human again—and oddly, he was sorry to have missed the change—sprawled naked on the sandy floor of a huge tube of metal.

The playground, he remembered. *The park. Leon!* Had all that really happened?

Someone was still licking his balls, though quick, teasing licks were beginning to sneak up onto the base of his shaft. Cory groaned and reached between his legs to put his hand on Leon's head. Leon looked up, his smile wry, and turned his head to kiss the inside of Cory's wrist before he returned to his slow, wonderful torture of Cory's cock.

Cory groaned, and Leon laughed. "You'll have to keep it quiet," he said softly. "There could be early joggers out."

"Joggers. Right," Cory panted, writhing until Leon took pity and resumed his attentions. "Does this mean we're... I don't know. Mated for life or something?"

Leon was ever-so-gingerly nibbling his way up the underside of Cory's cock. He paused to snort indelicately. "Even real wolves don't always mate for life," he said, punctuating each word with a nip and a lick. "That's a myth. And we're humans at heart. As shifters..." He stopped entirely to look soberly at Cory. "We're better at it than most humans. You'll have a good idea, from scent, whether someone is a good match for you, but there's no mystical force forcing you to act on it. Shifters change their relationships all the time. There's no reason we have to see ourselves as together forever, but I can promise this is no one-night stand." Leon smirked suddenly. "But you're getting a bit ahead of the game. This, right now? Is neither more nor less than the best blowjob you've ever had."

Also the only one, Cory did not say, because Leon's mouth was closing over his cock and he never wanted it to end.

There was warmth and wetness and Leon's tongue was pressing and stroking, his teeth just grazing the sensitive flesh enough to keep Cory dancing on a knife's edge of pleasure and pain, holding off his climax but dragging him inexorably toward it, like the tide coming in, waves rushing in and out.

Joggers, Cory thought, barely coherent. *Quiet.* He stifled his moans, but it only made the sensations more intense. He couldn't even move, because that might pull Leon's mouth away from him. His arms flailed, seeking purchase, something he could use to brace himself.

A finger slipped down the inside of Cory's thigh, past Leon's too-talented mouth, and pressed, gently but firmly at Cory's perineum. The pressure was too much for Cory's already overloaded system, and stars exploded behind his eyes as he came, groaning from behind gritted teeth.

When his vision cleared, Leon was looking smug and satisfied. "I've been wanting to do that to you for *months*," he admitted. He smiled down at Cory. "You look... delectable, lying there all debauched and rumpled like that. It makes me wish I'd brought lube, so I could finish the job right."

Cory blushed furiously, but didn't try to cover himself. "Too much sand," he said. "Ow."

"True," Leon sighed, then brightened. "We can go back to my place, once we're dressed again, and take a shower. Get rid of all that pesky sand. Find some lube."

"And a condom," Cory agreed. "I'm sold. Hand me my pants."

Leon passed over the pants, but shook his head. "Too late for the condom. Wolves can't roll rubbers."

Cory bit his lip, and Leon leaned in to kiss him. "Relax, okay? If either of us had a disease, we'd have smelled it. But if it makes you feel better, we can go down to the clinic this afternoon for the full round of tests."

"All right." Cory sighed, then glanced sideways. Leon's cock was still hard, jutting up out of a nest of soft, dark curls toward his well-toned stomach. Would it feel as good as it had when they'd been wolves? Cory's own cock, despite recent satisfaction, twitched. He grinned and began to pull his pants on faster. "Come on," he said. "Shower. Lube."

Leon chuckled. "You're awfully eager for a man who wanted to stay in the closet only twelve hours ago," he teased.

Cory laughed, too, a little self-consciously. "Yes, well, you took away all my masks. Now that you're faced with the real me, I expect you'll run screaming within a week."

Leon's hands cupped Cory's face, made him stop buttoning his shirt and look up into those deep brown eyes. "I've always known what you are," Leon said seriously. "I just had to make you see it, too."

Annual Full Moon Werewolf Ball
By Sean Michael

Annual Full Moon Werewolf Ball.

Grammercy snorted at the sign. It was a bunch of people pretending to be fantasy creatures. Some wore full body costumes, others just masks and tails. At midnight, according to the sign, they went out and had a "howling."

It was a romanticized, unrealistic, silly ball. These masked werewolves had no idea what it was like to be a werewolf.

Gramm was different.

The face he wore under the wolf mask was not so different from said mask. It'd been that way for just over a year. One bite from some random hook-up had changed his life forever. That first full moon... Shit, there had been nothing romantic about the first time he'd changed.

He had it under control now, more or less. He knew when it was coming, knew where to go not to get into trouble when it overtook him. Still, it kept him away from people, especially at night. Here he could let his wolf hang out and nobody would look twice. Maybe he could even hook up.

He paid his cover charge and stalked into the place, the driving beat hitting him immediately and calling to the feral beast inside him. He pushed into the crowd, men, women, all dressed up as wolves gyrating against him.

Gyrating.

Christ on a crutch. He might be desperate but he wasn't this desperate. Why had he come again?

The music got faster, and he could smell need, arousal, heat. It was going to make him fucking crazy and he couldn't decide if he wanted to just revel in it or get out.

That was when he smelled it.

Another male. Another familiar male. That little fuck who had bitten his thigh a year ago. Gramm was going to kill the bastard.

He scanned the room, cursing all the fucking wolf masks. No way was he going to be able to pick the guy out of the crowd just by looking. He was going to have to do it by scent.

He stilled, blocking out the bodies writhing against his own, closed his eyes and tilted his head back. With his nose working overtime and his mouth slightly open, he pulled in all the scents around him, trying to isolate the other real werewolf.

Rich, spicy, with a hint of whiskey and a wash of sex—the man was here. Grammercy hadn't even known his fucking name. All he'd thought with was his cock. The guy had been perfect. Wanton and needy, lean and hungry for him. He'd thought the biting had just been a part of that. He'd been fucking wrong, but now he could confront the guy and beat the shit out of him.

He made sure he had the scent solidly in his nose, then squared his shoulders and began pushing his way through the crowd. Gramm caught sight of him—long dark hair, bright green eyes, a huge scar on one cheek. That was new. Maybe the man had bitten someone who bit back.

Sights set now, Gramm stalked his prey, pushing past the people playing at being wolves. The guy was sliding through the crowd, moving faster, avoiding him. The fucker knew exactly who he was. It made him growl, low in his throat.

"God, that's hot." A little guy in a Wile E. Coyote mask pushed against him, began rubbing.

He growled louder, pushing Wile E. Coyote back into the guy behind him and curving to the left in an attempt to cut his prey off. He saw his prey slide a mask on, duck down, and then he was gone.

Fuck a god damned duck.

Gramm headed for the door, trying to pick up either a sight or a scent. Nothing. Damn it.

"Why are you back?" He couldn't tell where the voice came from, only that he heard it, heard some sort of accusation in it.

Snarling, he spun, looking for the speaker. Where the hell was he hiding?

The smells in the hall were more muddled, the breeze from the air conditioning taking them, diluting and twisting them. He growled, the hair on his arms standing up. A soft rumble answered him, then the door to the ballroom opened again, the light blinding him.

He put his arm out, eyes closing to slits as he took a couple of steps backward.

"Sorry. Sorry." A couple—the woman in leather, the man in a leash and a mask and little else—came out, laughing. "We were looking for a place to play."

He swallowed, the scent of them strong, masking everything else. God damn it. God damn it. He deserved his pound of flesh. At the very least he fucking deserved to know *why*.

He pushed his way back into the ballroom, but the place was more crowded than ever, and his senses were wide open, the sights and sounds and scents overwhelming now. Grunting, he tried backing up.

"Easy. Easy, you'll wolf out. The normals will freak." Gentle hands turned him, moved him toward the big double doors.

He pulled away from the hands on him, but the touch and the words were enough to have made everything back off and he could handle it again. That's when he realized the voice and the hands belonged to the guy who'd bitten him. He whipped around to see the son of a bitch, but the man was gone again.

"What the hell?" He shouted it, not caring what looks he got, and stormed down the hallway, nose working overtime. He was going to pick up the son of a bitch's scent again if it was the last thing he did.

The hotel was quieter, everyone not in the party heading out for the evening, into the late summer warmth. He kept following the scent, stumbling down the hall. As he reached the lobby, the smell got stronger, sharper. He narrowed his eyes and checked it out carefully.

There was a lean man heading up in the elevator, the fancy metal grate sliding down. That was fucking him. The guy.

Gramm headed in that direction. "Hold the elevator!"

"I don't think so, stud. You have danger in your eyes." The doors closed.

Son of a bitch.

Gramm went for the stairs, flying up them and shoving through the door, making his way to the elevator to see if the guy got off on that floor. It took him seven floors before it worked, the doors opening, the man stepping out, mask in hand, heading down the hallway.

Gramm stalked after him, breathing in deep, taking in that scent. It was him. He'd recognize that scent anywhere, even if he hadn't realized he was taking it in when he'd been bitten.

A key card was out, the man moving faster. If this guy

thought he was going into his room alone, he had another think coming. Gramm, at the very least, deserved some answers.

"Back off. I'm not interested in playing tonight." The man spoke without looking at him.

"I'm not playing. I want some fucking answers." He wasn't letting this asshole just disappear again.

"Answers to what?" The guy actually stopped, looked at him.

It startled Gramm into stopping, too. "You bit me."

Damn, this guy was a looker. No wonder Gramm had gone home with him. Lean and dark, eyes bright, pointed features—he was gorgeous.

"You were driving me crazy. You made me toothy. You know how we are."

"I didn't at the time." He snarled the words out, started stalking again.

"You didn't what?" There was honest confusion in the man's face.

"I didn't know how *we* are—how *you* were. You bit me and left me like this and without a fucking manual."

"What the hell are you talking about? Are you trying to suggest I turned you queer? Seriously?" The guy flipped him off. "Fuck off."

"What?" Jesus Christ, queer? Gramm had been queer all his damn life. He'd only been a werewolf the last eleven and some months.

"Look. You wanted to get all Alpha and hump me like a naughty puppy? Fine. That was fine. Hell, I let you spank my ass, even. I'm easy, but don't pretend that you didn't know you were queer."

"That's not what I'm talking about and you know it!" He was nearly screaming the words at the guy and several people in the hall gave him dirty looks.

"You've lost your mind. Go find a normal to fuck

with." The guy sneered at him, clearly not impressed with his anger, his yelling.

"Open the fucking door so we can do this in relative privacy. Unless you want me sharing our little secret with everyone here."

"You're the one in the mask, honey." The guy opened the door, slipping inside.

He pushed forward into the room, letting the door close behind him. He tore off his mask, tossing it aside. "You remember what I'm talking about now?"

"No." The weird part was, it smelled like the truth.

Gramm breathed in hard. This was the guy, he was sure of it. A hundred percent sure. "Then why did you run from me?"

"You're hunting. You're an Alpha. What am I supposed to do?"

"An Alpha? What the fuck are you talking about?"

The guy peered at him. "Are you drunk?"

Gramm growled and advanced on the asshole. "I am not fucking drunk. You fucking bit me and I want to know why the hell you did it."

"We were having sex! That's what we do!"

He shook his head. "I only ever had sex with you once, how the hell do we have a 'what we do'?" He was getting more fucking frustrated by the second.

The guy stamped one foot. Hard. "What? Is this some fucking Alpha trial thing? You came onto me. You smelled good. You fucked me. It was good. You know we mate for life and obviously you weren't into it. It would be stupid to do it again!"

"What the hell are you talking about?" This guy was insane. Which would explain the fucking biting. "You fucking *bit* me and I turned into a fucking werewolf!"

The man's head tilted. "That's a myth."

"A fucking myth?" He stalked forward and grabbed

the guy's lapels, started backing him up. "A fucking myth? I'm a goddamn werewolf thanks to you. Don't tell me it's a myth."

"You're fucking crazy! Like I couldn't smell it on you!"

"There was nothing to smell." He shoved the guy hard, pushing him back onto the bed.

"Bullshit. Bullshit. What is this? Why are you doing this? I left you alone!"

"That's fucking right you did! You bit me and changed me and left me to deal with it on my own." He stared down at the man on the mattress, wanting to just shake him.

"But that's impossible. Biting doesn't infect humans." The guy looked at him like he was insane. "It never has."

"Here I am. Living fucking proof. You bit me. You changed me. And you just disappeared."

"You didn't... Quit fucking with me!"

Gramm pounced the guy, straddling his waist, hands on his shoulders. "You quit fucking with me!"

"You're crazy. No wonder you didn't know."

"That werewolves are real? How the hell should I have known?" This guy was fucking with him.

"Because you are one?" Now he could smell fear.

The guy was fucking with him because he was scared. Okay. Okay, that was less insane. "I am now. I wasn't when we met." He growled, not letting up.

"That's a fucking myth, man! It doesn't work that way!"

He shook his head. "I'm on to your game. You're trying to make me think I'm crazy so I won't blame you."

"Blame me for what?" The guy surged up under him, bucking him off. "Look. You aren't interested. I get it. Fine. Leave me alone!"

He growled, pushing the guy back down, holding him down with his whole body this time. "I want to know

183

why you fucking did it!"

"Did what?" Teeth flashed. "You can't make someone a werewolf! Everyone knows that!"

"Everybody knows that werewolves don't fucking exist!" he countered.

"Oh, fuck off." The guy shoved hard at Gramm. "Just stop it."

"Stop *what*? You stop it! You fucking bit me. You bit me. You. Bit. Me." What was wrong with this guy?

"Yeah. I thought. So you don't want to be mates. That's cool. I left, okay?"

"What?" Gramm just... What?

"I thought...you were giving clear signals and obviously you didn't think it worked for you. Cool, but don't bitch."

He sat back up, just straddling the guy again. "I don't know what the fuck you're talking about."

"What Pack raised you? You're, like, giving off weird signals."

"Pack? Signals? Stop it. Make sense." Gramm was thoroughly confused, his anger drowning in it.

"You first."

"I *am* making sense. We hooked up almost a year ago. You bit me. I turned into a werewolf. I know they aren't real, yet here I am. And I can tell by your scent—now, I couldn't smell nearly this well before you bit me—that you're one, too. Why did you do it? Why did you bite me and make me like you and then just disappear to figure it out on my own?"

"It doesn't work that way! You can't turn a human. That's a MYTH!" Those beautiful eyes stared him down. "We don't mate with humans, we don't fuck them. They smell weird!"

Gramm shook his head. "You let me fuck you." He'd been there—there had definitely been a lot of fucking happening and this guy hadn't been in the least bit weirded out by the way he smelled.

"Exactly!"

"But you just said you don't mate with humans." This guy was insane. He had to be. It was the only answer that made any sense at all.

"No. We don't."

"But I was human when we hooked up!" He got up, started pacing the room. He was going to get as crazy as this guy was if the jerk didn't stop talking in circles.

"No, you weren't. You couldn't be. We don't mate with humans and..." The man sighed. "What do you want?"

"What do I want?" That had him stopping, standing there to stare. He didn't know. Answers, maybe. "I want to know why you did it."

"Did what?"

"Bit me! Turned me into a werewolf!" Had this guy been paying no attention at all?

"I didn't turn you into anything! I can't!"

Gramm crossed his arms over his chest. "Then explain to me how come I became a werewolf after you bit me."

"You didn't. You can't. You're either one of us or you're not."

Gramm shook his head. He was beginning to feel like a damn record stuck in one spot. "But I wasn't one of you...of us, until you bit me!"

"Stop it. Just stop it."

Gramm realized, suddenly, he didn't even know this man's name. "What's your name?" he demanded.

"Damien. What's yours?"

"Grammercy."

"Grammercy." When Damien said his name, he stepped forward, drawn.

There was just something about the man. There had been that night, too, the one where they'd come together.

When Damien had bitten him. He wanted. No. No, he fucking needed.

He pushed Damien back onto the bed and straddled him again. Only this time, he wasn't intending to yell.

"What are you doing?" Damien's body knew exactly what he was doing.

He ground against Damien's cock. "I'm doing this."

"No. No, I can't. You don't want to." Damien's body responded eagerly, easily.

"I want to just as much as I did that night. Maybe more." He rolled against Damien again, proving his words.

Damien groaned, arched beneath him.

"See? You can, too." He rolled again, rubbing them together.

The scent of Damien stunned him, made his mouth water. Groaning, he brought their mouths together. His. He snarled. This flavor was for him. He'd never felt this way before and he didn't care; he just needed to impress himself on Damien. He needed to make the man beg, to touch every inch.

He could feel the animal in him rising up, demanding that he make Damien yield to him. He dragged his nails down Damien's belly, loving how the man moved underneath him. The warmth of the skin and muscles beneath his fingertips made him moan. He bit at Damien's bottom lip, tugging when the man growled.

The word "mine" snarled through him and the only reason he didn't give it voice was because his mouth was busy. He tangled his fingers in soft fabric at Damien's throat and pulled, hard. The buttons on Damien's shirt popped, the noise satisfying.

"Asshole." Damien bit his lip hard enough to sting.

"Fuck you." Gramm bit back.

"You wish."

Like Damien wouldn't let him in. "I think it's you who wishes." Gramm rubbed his cheek against Damien's, just following his instincts.

"Not getting into this with you again."

He growled. "Into what?" He'd just been rubbing cheeks with the asshole.

"Mating." The word was growled back. "Mating, okay? You're obviously not in a place to do it."

"What the fuck? How do you go from a hook up to mating?" He was going to beat Damien like he'd planned from the start.

"You don't." Damien slipped out from under him in a move so fast he didn't even see it, then a sleek black wolf crashed out a window, out onto a balcony, and then he sprang out to the next one over.

"What the hell?" Gramm could only put down what happened next to utter shock and surprise.

He shifted himself, and leapt out after Damien, giving the wolf chase.

Damien moved like a shadow, fearless, perfectly brave, and beautiful. It made him want to howl. Jumping from balcony to balcony, Damien finally reached the ground and began to sprint. Once he was down, Gramm was able to pick up speed and shorten the distance between them. Damien was almost half his size.

He moved faster, began herding Damien toward his place. It was easier than he'd feared, to encourage Damien to move. It was almost like Damien wanted to do what Gramm wanted.

Slipping into an alleyway, Damien tried to escape him. Gramm wasn't going to let Damien get away, though. Not this time. Damien had started this, but Gramm was going to finish it.

Damien reached the end of the alley, a fence there blocking the way. Gramm vocalized happily—he had Damien now.

Damien crouched, faced him. Gramm let his teeth show and growled softly. Damien was his and would submit. The thought shocked him. It also turned him on, almost impossibly.

He wanted to whine and rub, but instead he growled again and advanced. Damien scooted back, teeth flashing, eyes rolling. He kept moving toward Damien, refusing to back away. He wasn't letting this one get away again.

The lean muscles tensed, and he knew Damien was going to leap. He knew it. He jumped at the same time and they went down together, his teeth around Damien's neck. He didn't break the skin, though; he was careful. He held on, growling deep, his body knowing exactly what to do. He was waiting for Damien to submit.

The lean body shook, then slowly eased, like it should. The tenor of his own growls changed as he let Damien know he was pleased. Good pup. Good mate. He shook gently, side to side. He didn't know exactly what was going on, but he was following his instincts and everything in him said this was right, good. As it should be.

His mate. The thought vibrated inside him like a prayer.

There was a noise from the street and he let Damien go, growled and nudged the wolf. They had to get off the street so he could take his mate. He herded Damien to his place, nipping and snapping at the wolf's heels.

They shifted together as they hit the front porch, and he let them in with the key from under the flower pot. He didn't even take the time to lock the door before he was on Damien, pushing the man up against the wall as he took his kiss. He didn't give Damien time to speak, he just fucked the man's lips.

His hands grabbed hold of Damien's arms, fingers digging in as he held on.

His.

He kept Damien still, fucking those sweet, open lips as hard as he could. When he found himself blindly humping their bodies together, he started moving them, pushing Damien toward the stairs as they continued kissing. Damien was hard as a rock, fucking his thigh.

The urge to tell Damien he was a very good naughty puppy was huge. He didn't. He just dragged the man all the way to his bed. Damien stumbled along behind him, cock hard and long, wet-tipped. Gramm tossed the man onto the bed, grinning wickedly when Damien bounced.

"I'm not staying here."

"You're staying." He straddled Damien—here they were again only this time they were naked, hard, and ready to go at it.

"Am not."

He leaned down, his teeth finding Damien's throat again. His. He growled as he bit. Loudly.

Damien cried out, bucking hard underneath him. He growled again, softly this time before raising his head and looking down at Damien. Damien's eyes were glowing, shining at him. He felt his response deep inside and he crashed their mouths together again. Damien's lips split, the coppery tinge of blood sharp on his tongue.

Growling, he drove their hips together. He scrabbled for Damien's leg, dragging it up along his thigh. Then he did the same with the other and shifted, his prick pushing at Damien's hole, demanding entrance. Damien's body was made for him; he knew this like he knew he needed to breathe.

Gramm pushed and Damien let him in, almost pulled him in, the head of his cock pushing through. There was no resistance, nothing but the sensation of coming home. It made him want to cry out, to scream—to howl.

He started fucking Damien, pushing in hard with every stroke. Later he would play; now he simply needed. He moved harder, faster, pounding into Damien's sweet hole. Damien's body met every thrust, body rippling madly.

He brought their mouths back together again, taking the kiss as surely as he was taking Damien's body. Damien's flavor exploded inside him, making him growl and snarl.

He finally gave voice to the feeling running through his veins. "Mine."

"Liar." Damien twisted underneath him.

He snarled and slammed in harder.

Damien grabbed his shoulders, cried out. "Please."

He wrapped one hand around the man's cock and pulled in time with his thrusts. He felt Damien's need, all around his prick. Hot. Needy. Desperate. He'd never felt anything like, the intensity was amazing. Perfect.

He gritted his teeth and moved faster, slamming into Damien. "Mine." He growled the word out with every thrust.

"Mate." Damien whispered the word.

"Yes." He hissed the word. That was right. Damien was his.

Damien's eyes went even wider. "Yes?"

"Yes. Mine." He bent and took another kiss, his hips shifting as he thrust in at a different angle.

He wasn't sure what he'd done, but it didn't matter. He knew what was what. He could feel it deep in his bones. He squeezed Damien's cock tight as he felt a growl growing deep in his belly. Damien's sound answered him, deep and needy, filling the air.

He would never let this man go. The truth in that rocked him to the core, and he felt his orgasm rise up from his balls.

"Harder. Harder. Let me feel you."

He squeezed Damien's cock again and again and pounded in, giving it all to the man under him. Damien's body gripped him, jerking around his prick.

"Come on. Show me how good it is."

Seed sprayed over his fingers, splashing down on Damien's belly. He did howl now, slamming into Damian and filling that ass with his seed. Marking Damien, deep inside.

He bent and bit at Damien's lower lip, then sucked on it. Those eyes stared at him, watched him closely. He stared back, still buried deep, buried right where he belonged.

A soft, curious growl sounded.

He answered with a single word, "Mate."

"Mate." Damien nodded, eyes glowing, shining at him.

It felt so fucking right.

He slipped out of Damien and settled on his back, pulling the man close to him.

"Are we going to fight again?" Damien sounded... cautious.

"I... Maybe." He chuckled. "I kind of like where it led this time."

Damien rumbled, hand swatting his ass.

He growled and grabbed Damien's hand. "I still have questions, though."

"Questions about what?"

"I still want to know why you did it."

"Why I did what?"

"Bit me." He held tight to Damien, not willing to have the man take off on him again. He was getting to the bottom of this. "I mean why do that? And then why try to make like you didn't do it to me?"

"We bite our mates. Mark them. I already apologized. You acted like I was your mate." There wasn't an ounce of deception in Damien's scent, in the words.

"I just don't understand how you could have thought I

was your mate before you bit me—I was just an ordinary human, then." Okay, maybe an exceptional human; he'd always excelled at everything he did and had never thought of himself as "ordinary".

"There's no way. I told you. We don't have sex with humans. Ever. It's all scent-based. I couldn't have been aroused by you if you weren't wolfy."

"But I wasn't a wolf until you bit me!" Gramm took a deep breath—he could tell Damien wasn't trying to wind him up, but he was telling the truth, too.

Damien shook his head. "I don't understand."

"Neither do I. You're telling me you thought I was already a wolf, and I'm telling you I wasn't. I know I'm not lying and I don't believe you are either, but we can't both be right."

"No. No, we can't. Your parents aren't wolves?"

"I was in the foster system. I don't know who my real parents are."

"So they were wolves." Damien nodded. "There you go. You just never had anyone activate your hormones. At least that sounds a little logical."

"Never had anyone activate my hormones... You realize that sounds insane?" This whole fucking thing was insane. Getting turned into a werewolf—still a fantastical creature the last time he checked, even if he now was one himself—mating by scent and feeling, these things weren't real. They didn't just happen.

Except here they were.

"Does it?" Damien shrugged. "It sounds pretty logical to me."

"Well. You've believed in werewolves your whole life. I didn't know they were real when I became one."

"That's crazy, man. You always *were* one. You just didn't know." Damien sounded so sure. It sort of made Gramm want to beat the man.

"You don't know that." How could he have always been a werewolf and never known?

"Well, what other answer is there? We don't turn people. You could bite anyone and they'd just be sore."

"So you say." And maybe that was the answer, but how could he have been a werewolf his whole life and never known?

"Well, I guess you could go try it. Go try and have sex with a human. You can't, can you?"

He growled at Damien. How had the fucker known?

"What? I told you. We can't have sex with humans."

"I had plenty of sex before you bit me." How could he have been a werewolf all his life? It kept coming back to that, over and over. He was aware he was pouting now, but couldn't help it.

"Well, then, go have sex some more. You obviously got fucked over by me." Damien rolled away, stalking toward his bedroom door.

"Stop right there." He growled at Damien. This man wasn't walking out on him.

"I'm leaving." He noticed that Damien had stopped, though.

"No, you aren't. Not because of some slight that never happened. I never said you fucked me over." He went over and grabbed Damien's arm, pulled him in close. "I don't understand how this happened, but it did and you're mine and if you run, I will hunt you to the ends of the earth."

Damien's eyes went wide, staring at him, and it was like time stopped.

"What?" Gramm demanded, growling hard.

"Nothing. Nothing."

He kept growling, low in the back of his throat. "What?"

"Nothing!" Damien pulled away. "I've been wanting

to... You left and... Fuck."

He pulled Damien back in, kissed the man until they were both panting. "Tell me."

"You're my mate. I've been stuck wanting you for a year."

"So why didn't you come get me?" He wouldn't wait a year to go get Damien if the man left him. He wouldn't wait a day.

"You didn't want me."

He blinked, frowned. "Why did you think that?"

"What? It was obvious. You didn't... You left. You weren't wanting me."

"It was a one-night stand and I was feeling sick. I didn't fucking know!"

"Neither did I. I thought you were just...saying it wasn't good enough." Damien spoke softly, not looking at him.

"Well I'm being pretty clear tonight."

Those eyes met his again. "Yeah."

He was going to tear Damien up. "Then there'll be no more talk of leaving." It wasn't a question. He walked them back over to the bed and tugged Damien down onto it.

"Why were you at the party?"

"Because I needed, and I knew I needed a wolf." He snorted. "Like any of those pretenders were wolves."

"There were four of us there tonight. Allie and her mate, Justin, and us."

"That's five," he teased. He hadn't realized there'd been any other wolves but himself and Damien. He should have known, though, right?

Damien chuckled. "Once you walked in, you were all I could smell."

That made him happy and he smiled at Damien. "This possessive feeling isn't going to go away, is it?" He wasn't complaining, it was hot.

"Never. We're mated."

"Are you okay with that?" He hadn't given Damien a whole lot of choice, hunting the man down and dragging him home as he had.

"We're mated." Like it was easy as that.

"I don't know much about being a wolf," he warned. He was bad at it. He'd had nearly a year to prove that.

"I don't know anything about not being one."

"That I know lots about."

Damien chuffed softly. "I'm only interested in learning about you, right now."

He rolled onto Damien, rubbing their hips together. "Ditto." They could figure out what the hell had happened later.

What was important right now was his mate and learning what was behind the masks they wore.

Masks Off!

Contributors' Bios

Elizabeth Brooks lives with her husband and two children in Virginia, where she masquerades as an uptight quality manager by day while writing gleefully smutty stories by night. When she's not writing or editing, she loves reading, roleplaying games, photography, and geeky gadgets of all sorts. You can find her online at http://EveryWorldNeedsLove.blogspot.com.

Charlie Cochet is a passionate author of M/M Historical Romance who loves to get lost in eras long gone, especially the Roaring Twenties and Dirty Thirties. From Prohibition agents to hardboiled detectives, speakeasies to swanky nightclubs, there's bound to be plenty of mischief for her heroes to find themselves in, and plenty of romance, too!

When she isn't writing, she can usually be found reading, drawing, or watching movies. She runs on coffee, thrives on music, and loves to hear from readers. Find out more about Charlie and her writing on her website: www.charliecochet.com, or visit her blog: www.charliecochet.blogspot.com

Missouri Dalton is a writer of horror/paranormal contemporary fantasy and alternate historical novels.

Missouri was raised mainly in transit, slowed down

to finish school in one place and was then determined to be as nomadic as possible, if only because that's how things just worked out. She uses writing as an escape from her own neurosi and currently lives with her dear friend Sophia.

The nickname "Queen of Happy Endings" is an apt one for **Katherine Halle**. She firmly believes that no matter what the obstacles, what the struggles, or how much angst is involved in the journey that the ending should always be a happy one.

Katherine's love of the written word started at a very early age with repeated demands of "read to me" to any who would listen. It was only natural that writing would follow. As a child, she could often be found daydreaming, thinking up fanciful stories and writing them down. Now she does it on a laptop. Much faster.

Katherine can be found online at http://www.katherinehalle. wordpress.com/blog/ or on twitter @ KatherineHalle.

Often referred to as "Space Cowboy" and "Gangsta of Love" while still striving for the moniker of "Maurice," **Sean Michael** spends days surfing, smutting, organizing an immense gourd collection and fantasizing about one day retiring on a small secluded island peopled entirely by horseshoe crabs. While collecting vast amounts of vintage gay pulp novels and mood rings, Sean whiles away the hours between dropping the f-bomb and pursuing the kama sutra by channeling the long lost spirit of John Wayne and singing along with the soundtrack to "Chicago."

Check out Sean's webpage at http://www.seanmichael writes.com/

Rob Rosen, author of the novels "Sparkle: The Queerest Book You'll Ever Love", "Divas Las Vegas", "Hot Lava", "Southern Fried", and "Queerwolf", has had short stories featured in more than 150 anthologies. Please visit him at www.therobrosen.com

BA Tortuga enjoys indulging in the shallow side of life, with hobbies that include collecting margarita recipes, hot tub dips, and ogling hot guys at the beach. A connoisseur of the perverse and esoteric, BA's days are spent among dusty tomes of ancient knowledge, or, conversely, surfing porn sites in the name of research. Mixing the natural born southern propensity for sarcasm and the environmental western straight-shooting sensibility, BA works to produce mainstream fiction, literary erotica, and fine works of pure, unadulterated smut.

With characters ranging from supernatural demons to modern-day cowboys, alternative illustrated men to Victorian dandies, the addiction to history and atmosphere is ever present, and laced through with sensual pleasure. BA's latest projects include werewolves, rodeo cowboys, and fistfighting rednecks.

Find BA at http://www.batortuga.com/

Masks Off!

CPSIA information can be obtained at www.ICGtesting.com
Printed in the USA
BVOW011001050413

317414BV00012B/332/P

9 781610 403528